REMNANT
RESISTANCE

—— *by* ——

STEPHEN BAMBROUGH

authorHOUSE®

AuthorHouse™ UK
1663 Liberty Drive
Bloomington, IN 47403 USA
www.authorhouse.co.uk
Phone: 0800.197.4150

Published by AuthorHouse 04/01/2016

ISBN: 978-1-5246-3022-5 (sc)
ISBN: 978-1-5246-3023-2 (hc)
ISBN: 978-1-5246-3024-9 (e)

Contents

Prologue

Barely able to keep my weary eyes open, I was completely exhausted both physically and mentally. I wish I could say there were some insightful thoughts going through my head but, truth be told, my only thought was to get to a bed and fall asleep for three or four days straight. Griffin Holster, Remnant killer and saviour of the world – it has a nice ring to it. If the world found out that would probably be the news headline, along with the help of my companions of course, Bill, Jess and Jasper... The thought of Jasper instantly brought my mood down. I felt responsible; I had no control over the situation and now he was gone, just like that, gone.

Everyone had gone quiet as the makeshift vessel beached up on the shoreline on this sunny evening – at least I think it was evening, the stormy weather had been completely dispersed by the explosion of the capsule device. I had lost all sense of time. Across the horizon my blurred sight made out the outlines of a few people looking out and probably wondering about the strange lights in the sky that had occurred when I blew up the island. An elderly couple walking a small dog arrived next to the boat looking bewildered.

"Looks like you lot have all been through the wars" mentioned the old man becoming instantly concerned.

"Lizzy, call an ambulance will you, dear," he ordered before turning his attention back to us.

"Are you alright? Can you move?" he enquired.

I wish I could have answered him properly but in my destroyed state my brain was not functioning and all I could think about was why anyone would have a stupid little dog like theirs.

"I bet your dog's called Rex or Rover or something old like Albert." I laughed like an idiot. The man looked at me completely confused.

"Think you had better hurry with that ambulance, dear. I think the boy's lost his marbles," he called over to his wife.

Sirens alarmed seconds later as a set of blue flashing lights raced along the road and stopped next to the beach.

"Well, wasn't that fast?" said the woman looking surprised at the phone in her hands.

My eyes were almost completely shut when a couple of men raced along the beach from the ambulance until they were next to the boat.

"We'll take it from here thanks," one of the men told the elderly couple.

"Can you move? Speak?" asked the youngest looking man. As much as I wanted to I couldn't answer. I had had enough and closed my eyes, falling into blissful unconsciousness.

Chapter 1

All In The Past

I still look like the same person, apart from a couple of newly gained scars, and I still think in the same manner I did before recent events took a hold of my life. Perhaps I have gained a slight increase in confidence; I've certainly become increasingly grateful for the people around me, Jess and Bill in particular, and have found a new sense of responsibility to keeping them close and safe. Although saying this I do feel like my life has a new found meaning, I have actually become a person of usefulness – I have had a small epiphany in that sense. People may never find out what I had done but I knew, that is all that mattered. My name is Griffin Holster and I no longer feel like an ordinary man in an ordinary world.

To say the past few days have been a life changing experience would be an understatement. If I'm going to be completely honest I still struggle to believe the events which have transpired. The more I think about it the crazier it begins to sound. Remnant, Angious, Hesthenon, Helvius, and Terraforming capsules – it all equals madness, but I know it was real, I was there; I witnessed it with my own eyes and I survived it.

There was an awareness that I was in hospital, but I had been kept under constant sedation and spent most of my time sleeping and resting my wounds which were healing at an accelerated rate due to device on my arm.

Recurring nightmares plagued any sleep I could manage which achieved only to wake me up in a pool of sweat shaking at the vividness of the memories.

It was always the same setting. Me standing on top of the islands jagged cliff facing out onto the raging stormy sea. Lightning dominated the blackened skies as down below I spy Jasper struggling to stay afloat in the overwhelming ferocity of the swelling waves.

"GRIFFFF!!!"

Too far away to be of any help I scream at the top of my lungs at Jasper to swim to the nearby walkway next to the cliff face.

"SWIM, JASPER, GOD DAMNIT!!"

Helplessly watching on I see him reach the wooden walkway just for his body to be ripped back into the sea by the hands of the evil Lucifer, his face smirking up at me before he follows Jasper to the depths of the wild waters and they disappear from sight.

A cold and hostile hand perches on my shoulder. Turning my head I am met by the demonic gaze of those blue and red beady eyes of the Remnant just before it roars into my face with a horrific cry and its talons rip down, piercing my chest.

My eyes opened wider than imaginable as I struggled for breath, panting like I had never used my lungs before. There didn't seem like there was enough oxygen in the room to satisfy me and I became even more panicked, clutching my chest where the Remnant had ripped into me.

A gentle hand rested on my shoulder and, unlike the one in my dreams, it felt comforting and protective. Looking to my right I saw a man dressed in a brown suit.

"Steady yourself, Mr Holster. You have been through a great deal. We do not need you giving yourself a heart attack now," he said with a kind smile and the slightest hint of a German accent.

My state of panic began to recede and my vision came into focus. Taking a few deep rhythmic breaths I calmed to a more relaxed state. Looking up at this mysterious man I could take in more of his features. His hair was a sleek black and cut to a medium length weaving to the sides, his eyes were brown and supported on his face by a set of wrinkles where he had smiled or laughed too much. The square jawline was tipped off at the chin with a pointed small grey beard pulled up onto his face by his warming smile. I'm not entirely sure why, but the way he looked seemed to support his German accent, not that I usually like to stereotype.

Looking further around the room I needed to ensure I was still in the same place as when I closed my eyes. Everything was clean and white as the sun shone through the window blinds. Relief swept over me when I saw my ragged mucky clothes lying on the chair exactly where I had left them. The monitor next to my bed that was measuring my vitals began to steady and slow down from the alarming rate it had been recording a second ago.

Most people I have met seemed to have an irrational fear of hospitals, which I could not understand. I've always felt them comforting – it's a room designed to keep you healthy and safe with people looking after you twenty-four-seven. Ever since I had to have my tonsils out I've found them reassuring and have never really minded being an occupant.

"You've been sedated for quite some time, Mr Holster. I think it's about time you got back on your feet, don't you?" The man's voice interrupted my musings.

"Who are you?" I questioned. His smile grew bigger.

"Well, I'm glad you asked." He walked over to the end of the bed where he began casually pacing side to side.

"My name is Dr Dalton Meier and, before you ask, not the medical variety. You may have already guessed I am originally from Germany; I am still working on the accent. My age I hope I concealed slightly better at forty-two years young. I have an extremely generous IQ of one hundred and fifty-five. I am a member of the elusive Illuminati and of course my favourite colour... is blue." He listed his details tilting his head to one side.

He stopped still at the foot of my bed grinning at his own description. It took a brief second for me to click onto what he had just said.

"Wow, wow, wait a minute, pal! Did you just say the illuminati?" I asked sceptically raising a hand to indicate for him to slow down.

"Now, that I certainly did, Mr Holster. Rather mysterious organisation isn't it? Well I can assure you we mean nothing but the best in contradiction to some of the rather foul rumours lingering over our proud title."

"Foul rumours?"

Now, I'm no stranger to the stories of the illuminati but that's all they were to me – made up stories, fiction. Was it so hard to believe that they actually existed? Usually I would have waved him off as a mad man but following recent circumstances my mind was a little more open to the idea.

"Oh you know, all this controlling the world business. When actually we are protecting it, from an evil you yourself have already encountered."

"You're talking about the Remnant?" I asked, knowing full well it was exactly what he was talking about.

"Precisely! I mean don't get me wrong, Mr Holster, we are a rather powerful force working below the civilian radar, retaining complete anonymity. We own certain companies, which bring in the necessary funding for our group and we have what you might call, a free pass within every country." His face betrayed a certain amount of smugness.

"Our little group funded the moon landing with a little help from our researchers and some technology acquired which far surpassed anything we could have dreamed of at the time. That was our first encounter with one of the ancient devices, although sadly too large and too far away to be of any use to us," he explained further.

It was obvious he loved every second of this question and answer session. I frowned in his direction as he stood waiting at the end of the bed for a response. To be honest, I was willing to believe this man, but something inside me wanted to test him, the way he spoke was just unrealistic. I did enjoy listening to him but I felt the urge to break his smugness.

"Bullshit!"

He looked at me amused, pulling a small black torch from an inside pocket of his jacket. Lifting his right hand up with the palm facing me he shone a light half red, half blue directly up onto the centre of his hand. What I saw was pretty astounding. It was almost like a tattoo except it seemed to rise off from his hand like a hologram. The picture itself was the symbol I recognised as the Illuminati emblem, a pyramid encompassing an all seeing eye.

"OK, that is pretty cool, but it doesn't prove what you say is true," I insisted.

Raising an eyebrow at my determination he flicked the light away from his hand waving it side to side.

"The symbol represents two parts which you may recognise. The pyramid being the glass prism used to refract the portal information, the 'all seeing eye' is our moon, the source of said signal. The tattoo will only become visible under a certain spectrum of light to which all members carry."

Underneath the symbol were the words, Lebe Ein Lautes Leben Leise.

"What's the sentence mean?" I asked.

"It's German, young man and it translates to 'live a loud life quietly', our little group motto," he explained.

Swinging the torch around, he shone it down directly onto my hand. The same image lifted up in front of my eyes. I stared in amazement.

"Consider yourself an honorary member, Mr Holster. Obviously due to the sudden nature of your union we will have to discuss in more detail our arrangements another time. I can only imagine the things you discovered on that island and to be completely blunt with you, we need you and that device attached to you." He pocketed the small light source as he spoke and I had the uncomfortable feeling that he was more interested in the device than me.

"We arrived at the shore just as you and your companions arrived back to mainland. You made quite the scene. We were the ones that called the ambulance taking you to the hospital and, of course, we kept it all below the government's radar. It's all on a need to know basis right now. Your parents believe you are in police custody and we can certainly invent some other plausible alibi for the extended time you will be away. So, as you can see, Mr Holster, we have everything under control and you have nothing to worry about." He smiled at his control and insight over the situation.

"Nothing to worry about? I've apparently just joined the Illuminati and I think we both know there's going to be something to worry about," I replied.

Laughing at my comment he walked over to my side picking up a bundle of clothes from a table and dropping them on top of the bed.

"I took the liberty of acquiring a set of clothes from your home. You should get dressed as we will be setting off soon. There are Remnant to be rid of!"

Shuffling over to my old pile of clothes on the opposite side I picked up my tattered work jacket and rummaged in the front pocket for the letter I had brought back from the island.

"Don't worry. Mr Holland's letter has been sent to its rightful destination. I assure you, Mr Holster. We are the good guys."

I was relieved that the letter had reached Dave Holland's wife. After that whole dreaded experience on the island, I was glad I could change at least one person's life for the better by providing some closure.

"Thanks, it means a lot." I acknowledged his gesture beginning to let my guard down.

"It's quite alright. I will be waiting outside for you," he said with a nod before departing the room.

Then, once again, I was alone. Staring at the palm of my hand there was nothing to be seen by the naked eye. Everything was silent bar the rhythmic beat of the monitoring equipment. One of the nurses must have removed my anaesthetic drip while I was asleep as a small plaster covered the top of my wrist. My shoulder had been stitched up and bandaged which had been the main cause of grief during my stay on the island. Cuts and bruises on my face had surprisingly subsided in quantity. In fact, I was healing rather rapidly, and my thoughts were that the Nano-generators in my bloodstream might be helping the healing process along like a clotting agent but, then again, what did I know? I'm no doctor or scientist. Looking at my right arm the Angious wrist device was still firmly lodged in place. I had begun to stop noticing it as if it were just an extension of my limb.

Removing the monitoring pads from my body allowed me to sit upright on the side of my bed. Rolling my shoulders caused a large cracking sound loosening my joints having been stuck in the same position for days. Facing out the window I stood up and parted the white blinds to take a look outside. It was a sunny day and birds flew past in the clear sky as blue lights and sirens flared past. Outside it was just another normal morning.

Inspecting the clothes Dalton had chosen for me, I was more than happy with his choices: dark blue jeans, a plain black shirt and my favourite black leather jacket, accompanied by a pair of slightly worn trainers. I was never one for fashion, just comfort. My bandages were all clean and I believed I could probably do without them but the doctors must have their reasons so I pulled my clothes on over the top, concealing all injuries to my body. Actually I was feeling quite energetic; the few days of rest had worked wonders.

I took one last look at my pile of old ripped up work clothes on the bedside chair. That was the old Griffin Holster. With that final thought I headed through the door.

Chapter 2

A New Destination

"Griff!"

Jess's voice was a welcoming sound as I entered the plain hallway which reeked of disinfectant. Before I had any time to reply I was enfolded in her embrace. I flinched from surprise and expected a pain from my wounds. Luckily pain did not ensue.

"Alright, Jess, nice to see your smiling face again," I said with a smile of my own.

"Looks like I'm becoming a third wheel then," joked Bill, walking over from behind Jess who gave him a bit of a glare. I stepped away from Jess and gave Bill a firm handshake.

"Good to see you as well pal." I happily greeted the big brute although he squashed my hand with some force.

They were no longer wearing the coastguard uniform I had become so accustom to. In fact, both of them were wearing fairly normal clothes.

"It's good to see up again young'un, you've been talking some shite the past few days drugged up on your painkillers."

"So no different to usual then," I replied, smirking.

I had no recollection of anyone visiting me the past few days which was slightly concerning – they must have had me on a serious concoction of painkillers. Having him say that also made me think about Dalton. It had been a pretty weird conversation, could I have possibly been hallucinating?

"You haven't by any chance met that strange Dalton fella have you?" I asked.

"Yeah, strange is an understatement," answered Bill looking unimpressed.

"I like him, I think he's quirky," Jess said, smiling.

"Think you mean queer. But speak of the devil here's our man now," Bill pointed out, keeping his voice just low enough so as not to be heard by Dalton himself.

Dalton appeared from a stairwell down the hallway. I don't know why I doubted his existence. This whole experience must have made me unwillingly paranoid. At least seeing Bill and Jess in good health was reassuring, although the thought of never seeing Jasper again kept niggling the back of my mind.

"If you would all be so kind as to follow me we have work to do!" Dalton shouted down the hallway before disappearing back into the stairwell, some of the staff looked a little bemused before carrying on with their duties.

"We're going already? Jesus, I only just got up!"

"I don't know how you can complain. You've been napping this whole time. I've had to put up with that Dalton guy for the past few days and I haven't even had a single pint of ale since I got back," Bill moaned.

"If you're both finished complaining I think we're expected to go, so come on," said Jess, heading toward the stairwell.

"The lady has spoken," Bill mocked with a grin as we followed.

Passing various types of hospital equipment everything seemed so sterile and bright which was in complete contrast to the island where everything had seemed nightmarishly dark and dirty. Staff members chatted away to one another not knowing the evil which resides on our planet – they didn't have a clue. A small part of me sort of wished I still had that naivety myself, but that would make life too easy.

We passed one of the hospital food carts with trays neatly arranged ready to be sent into the wards for breakfast. I ended up quickly snatching one of the bananas doubting it would be missed.

"What happened to Kev?" I asked with a full mouth as we walked along the hallway.

"Plausible deniability. He didn't have a clue what happened on that island so we didn't have to get him involved. As far as he is concerned he was in a helicopter crash and was not clearly thinking from his injuries," explained Bill.

Wandering into the stairwell I heard footsteps up above and Dalton's head popped over the railings staring down at us.

"Anytime today would be brilliant!" he shouted in his strange fashion.

We climbed to the top where the metallic doors were gaping open. I could hear the helicopter blades whirring around before I had even exited the stairwell. There it was, unlike any helicopter I had ever seen. My knowledge on aircraft was pretty varied but the make of this one eluded me. As well as the two cockpit seats it had four more passenger places in the main compartment; it was shining black with sharp dynamic edges. I may not have known what it was but I knew I wouldn't have said no to one if offered as a gift.

"You like it, yes?" asked Dalton who had been waiting at the exit for us.

"Erm… yeah I do, what is it?" I asked in awe of this incredible machine.

"It's a modified Bell 407, created specifically for our needs and enhanced to be one of the fastest copters in existence. Being in our little organisation has its benefits." Dalton grinned. He was definitely a man who thrived when showing off.

"We could have done with one of these in the coastguard," Bill suggested with the same look of admiration.

A large black box was on the underside of the craft split into two length-way compartments.

"What's that on the bottom?" I questioned curiously.

"Countermeasures," Dalton replied. I assumed he meant some kind of flare device to prevent missile lock on. That was the only kind of countermeasure I knew about on an aircraft and it seemed a little over the top to me.

Boarding the vehicle we took our places in the comfortable matching black leather seats and the door was slammed shut by the co-pilot which cancelled out the loud noise created by the spinning rotors above. Dalton sat with his legs stretched out and crossed over while holding the back of his head with both hands in the most casual manner.

Gently lifting off we were on our way to our next destination. It didn't take long for us to distance ourselves from the shrinking urban setting below. It also didn't take long for my curiosity to kick in with the realisation I had just willingly followed this man to an unknown destination without a clue of his intentions. Possibly a little stupid on my behalf, but I guess as Bill and Jess had come along as well, there must be good reasoning behind his plans.

The prospect of having my adventure continue was too great an opportunity to give up. Maybe this time I will even get the girl I thought, looking over at Jess. She is quite feisty and sort of grows on you. I did like her more and more the longer I spent time with her. I moved my gaze away from her so as not to get caught staring. An awkward journey was the last thing I needed.

"Sooooo, where are we going exactly?" I asked.

"To the place beyond the forest to find another one of those Angious capsules and, with your newly acquired knowledge, destroy it!" Dalton said getting straight to the point.

"Wow! To be honest with you I don't know how much help I'm going to be with that. How do we know where to start anyways?"

Dalton leaned closer toward me and rested his hands on his knees.

"Well you see, Mr Holster, we recently found out that these devices which give off the time travel signal work on certain light wavelengths and when the wavelengths from the moon capsules collide with the wavelengths from the earth capsules they create a colour distortion. That is why when looking up to the moon I believe you probably saw a slight change in colour, yes?"

"Yeah, I saw that but how do you know this? I thought you hadn't seen a capsule properly?" asked Jess, joining in on the conversation.

"Indeed I have, Miss Hart. In fact the particular capsule I have seen had been causing us some rather annoying difficulties. I assume you all know by now the original function of the capsules, before they were sabotaged into time travel devices?" he enquired.

Terraforming the planet was its original function, drawing in nearby comets and asteroids to provide the necessary minerals and elements to support life once more after the collision of the planets. I remember this from Zarathus. We all nodded our heads in anticipation of the rest of his story.

"Well, the capsule I saw was hidden deep down in the Atlantic Ocean quite a few miles off the east coast of Florida. Being submerged at such large pressures must have damaged the capsule causing it to malfunction. In turn it must have falsely recognised passing ships and aircraft as mineral rich asteroids pulling them down into the sea. Of course this was extremely difficult to manoeuvre around but we eventually managed to cover the device up. With that we say goodbye to the whole Bermuda triangle mystery," he explained.

"Ha! I always knew it was aliens," Bill butted in comically.

It seemed like a lot of mysteries were explainable through the Angious and the Remnant. All the myths and stories through history seemed to be linked in some form to these creatures from the past who have been popping up every now and again. The three of them continued the conversation but my mind began to wander. Passing over open water below I half expected to see a flare rise up in the distance. Flying used to be a great pleasure of mine but now it had become a nervy experience thinking at any moment another one of those flying Remnant beasts would clash with the helicopter picking it out of the sky at its will. Again my mind turned toward Jasper and how he was lost for eternity somewhere in the depths below. I couldn't get him out of my head.

"Griff… are you with us?" asked Jess concerned, knocking me from my train of thought.

"Yeah, yeah. I was just thinking about everything that has happened," I answered with a hint of melancholy.

"You know, we all lost people we cared about on that island. Just think, if we manage to get rid of all the capsules we might be able to stop the same thing happening to anyone else ever again," she reasoned.

"I won't rest until all those bastards are gone, especially for what they did to Edmund," Bill added. I had forgotten about Edmund, Bill's friend being possessed and then disfigured by the hotel fire and eventually killed by Bill himself. I grieved for Jasper but I couldn't imagine killing him like Bill had had to do.

I guess we all felt an obligation to the people we lost to prevent recent events from happening again. There was no way I could go back to leading a normal tedious life after being part of something so extraordinary.

"Don't worry, Bill, I think we are with the right people to get the job done." I nodded toward Dalton who was listening in but keeping any smart replies to himself. He was obviously smart enough to realise when and when not to make any remarks as people's emotions boiled over.

"We must put an end to the invasion of these demonic creatures. One capsule at a time we will prevent them reaching our plane of existence. But we know destroying the capsules is only the beginning, to truly stop them we must somehow stop the transmission of the time code from the moon capsules and rid the planet from all existing Remnant," Dalton explained.

"Seems like a daunting task for a group of four," Jess pointed out.

"We have a whole organisation working across the globe to fight off this threat. Besides, we now have Mr Holster and his stupendous wrist device on our side."

That same old uncomfortable feeling once again surfaced, knowing people were relying on me. This person who I had never met before seemed to have complete faith in me, yet he had no knowledge of my existence until a couple of days ago. It was an uncomfortable feeling but I guess it was also a little reassuring that there were still people out there willing to believe in others.

"How exactly will I be of help anyway?" I enquired staring at Dalton inquisitively.

"Well I was informed by your companion, Miss Hart here, that you actually linked up to one of these capsule devices. Now if we can achieve this again you could give me the information you acquire which we could possibly even manage to translate. This may give us the means to defeating the Remnant.

"That and you are the only person we know of that has actually successfully destroyed a capsule, even if you did eviscerate an entire island in the process." he added, grinning.

"Wait, I thought you stopped the one under the water?" asked Bill.

"Stopped… not destroyed. To be completely honest with you we only covered it up as to stop it functioning," Dalton explained.

"You've been around for such a long time. How come you haven't figured out how to stop the portals yourselves?" I asked

"Well it was not through a lack of trying, my young friend. We had some of the greatest minds in history working with us, my personal favourite being Einstein." He grinned.

"You're telling me Einstein was in the illuminati? Well it's not the weirdest thing I've heard today," I conceded.

"O my yes. He was the closest to work out how the portals worked with his theories of special relativity and light travel, how people travelling at a speed of light may travel for seconds where observers see years. Fascinating really, but not quite on the ball."

Looking dumbfounded I was filled with even more questions. It was hard to know what to make of it all.

"Einstein in the illuminati! Next you'll be telling me Hitler was a Remnant," I joked.

"Ha, I'm afraid not. Hitler was a delirious, psychotic, power mongering racist, a monster in his own right but not of the variety you are thinking of! Now, Sir Adrian Carton de Wiart also known as the un-killable soldier is a different matter!" he said getting considerably louder and more excitable.

"The only Angious-possessed man we ever found who felt he owed us a debt at allowing him to survive in our time giving himself to us in the fight against evil, he was actually seriously wounded on eight occasions and participated in no less than three major wars including both world wars as well as surviving two plane crashes and escaped a POW camp. No normal human could achieve such an accomplished life and survive such extremes!"

"Some guy then, wasn't he?" I replied.

"Some guy indeed."

My brain had been battered with information and new history. It was a lot to take in. Everything I had ever known either was or could possibly be a lie.

Slouching back in my seat I stared back outside across the open waters. Somehow I think the adventurous lifestyle I always wished for wasn't all it was cracked up to be, full of responsibilities and loss as well as very little recognition. I bet if James Bond were real he would have been sick of his life although I definitely wouldn't be classed in the same category as him. Your Majesty's Secret Service would probably laugh at an average Joe such as me. At least he would have known where he was going, though. Somehow I feel my next destination was not going to be the whole family beach holiday to Spain I was accustomed to. No cocktails and beach football for me.

With the conversation subsiding I found my eyes slowly closing from the gentle rock of the helicopter. It was always the case when finding myself a passenger in a vehicle, to be able to drift off – no problem whatsoever.

It did not take long for the vivid nightmares to start plaguing my dreams once again. There I was hiding on my own behind some jagged rocks in the forest overlooking the ancient pyramid that I clearly remember destroying. Everything seemed even darker and hazier than my actual experience on the island. Red hooded figures emerged dragging Jess and Bill behind them, both tied up struggling and screaming. My conscience was commanding me to run out and do something to help but I remained frozen on the spot.

A second later, more hooded figures emerged with the prism and double circles on top of the poles – I knew what was coming. Held up to a height, the viscous black portal began to form on the side of the pyramid. One by one the large scaly Remnant creatures entered dragging their claws along the floor. The first of the monsters raised its arm and let out a blood curdling roar. I couldn't watch. My body unfroze and I turned around. Panic set in even more as a hooded figure appeared in front of me, removing his hood to reveal his face, blood running from his eye and chin. It was the possessed Michael, holding the large metal shard I had previously dug into his skull after attacking Jasper. Without hesitation he thrust the shard toward my face.

"Fucking hell!" I exclaimed waking up, shaking once again and holding my chest as it painfully contracted.

"Shit! Griff, are you alright, mate?" asked Bill alarmed.

Taking a few desperate deep breaths I found relief at seeing Bill and Jess next to me, although their faces showed grave concern.

"I'll be alright," I answered a little unconvincingly.

Outside had turned dark and we were flying above land – I must have been asleep longer than I thought. I looked upwards toward space and there it was, a purple hazed moon with a red glow emanating from all sides. Eventually my breathing returned to its original natural rhythmic pattern as I stared at the anomaly.

"We must be close, right? How do we know what to look for?" I asked. The concerned look on Dalton's face slowly subsided.

"Well we know that previous civilisations managed to contain the Remnant by constructing large structures around the capsules to prevent the time signal reaching the prisms above the devices. Structures such as pyramids," Dalton explained.

"Or maybe a castle?" suggested Jess, pointing out the window. Peeking out, I saw the large blackened outline of a castle standing atop a hill, overlooking a small village and surrounded by forest.

"Welcome…. To Romania," Dalton announced dramatically sweeping his arm across the window.

Chapter 3

Country, Castles, Calm

Wait a minute! Romania... Castle...

"Erm, what castle are we looking at exactly?" I asked Dalton.

"Why, the one and only Bran Castle," he answered excitedly.

I took another glance down as the outline became ever closer in the shadows of the night.

"Are you taking the mick?" I replied unbelievingly.

"Why? What's wrong with the place?" asked Bill confused.

"Bran castle, in Romania..." I said holding my hands up to him willing him to realise the significance of this place. Still clueless he shook his head. I placed my head in my hands in disbelief.

"It's Dracula's castle, Bill," informed Jess rolling her eyes.

Bill took another swift look outside then looked back at the two of us.

"Fuck right off," he replied. "I've agreed to come and fight some Remnant, but vampires as well... no way!"

"You do not have to worry about the undead, Bill. I assure you Remnant will be the only problems we may face. As a matter of fact, Bran Castle has absolutely nothing to do with the fictional vampire tale, not even to the extent of Vlad the Impaler who ruled in the fifteenth century," Dalton assured.

"You say don't worry but a week ago Angels and Demons were just stories to me, and a couple of days ago I had them trying to claw my bloody head off. I liked it better when it was only evil people I had to fight," Bill replied.

The helicopter made a smooth landing on an open patch of grassland not far from the castle itself.

"Well it's too late now, Bill," I said as the door slid open.

Stepping out from the warm comfort of the helicopter the fresh night breeze struck my face. It wasn't particularly freezing, just my body's reaction time being slow to accommodate the quick temperature change, although this didn't bother me, I am of course an Englishman.

Checking my wrist the red arrow of the Remnant indicator was unsurprisingly pointing toward the castle. That would be right; of course the monstrous demonic creatures would be hiding in the most cliché place.

Followed out by my companions Dalton was the last to exit the aircraft. Opening up a compartment hidden in the side of the helicopter he retrieved an array of weapons with flashlight attachments. To Jess and myself he handed a pair of pistols with the accompanying weapon holsters.

"I don't think we'll be doing much damage with these," I said mockingly.

"Not if you do not use it correctly. With a trained eye a perfect shot to the Remnant heart with these Heckler and Koch pistols will make short work of them. It's all about the aim not the amount or size of the bullets." Dalton corrected my attitude.

"Yeah, but I'm not exactly trained," I retorted.

"Well, hopefully you won't require its use."

Knowing that was probably the most unlikely outcome, I also knew there was at least one Remnant up there and where there is one, there is probably at least a handful, like rats – big, scaly, murderous rats.

A second later Dalton emerged with a larger rifle and placed it in Bill's hands.

"Bill, on the other hand, is trained and will probably be of more worth holding one of these. The SA80 I believe is the standard you are used to?"

Bill grew a smile across his face, weighing up the weapon.

"You're damn right, mate. This will do nicely," he answered, peering down the attached scope.

Ammunition was distributed evenly; a couple of clips to each person which snapped onto the belt.

We were then handed a small cubic object about 20mm in height and length and 10mm in thickness with two buttons on the side and a clip on the other.

"Communication for the masses," said Dalton as he slipped the cube onto his jacket. I followed suit and placed mine on my jacket collar.

"Hold one button to speak, one click of the other to mute, small, watertight to one hundred and fifty foot depth with a range of just over a mile. Simplicity, I love it," said Dalton.

One last rummage into the side compartment saw Dalton return with a large metallic case.

"What's in the box?" asked Bill.

"Just a prototype of a gadget I have been working on, which may come in handy," he answered cryptically.

"Alright, cheers pal, don't give me too much information," responded Bill sarcastically.

We began walking toward the direction of the castle and the helicopter floated back up into the air.

"Is he not waiting for us?" inquired Jess.

"Yes, but at a far safer location. Not to worry, Miss Hart, as soon as I make the call he will be back within fifteen minutes," Dalton replied.

"Hmm, alright then.".

"Well, no time like the present," urged Dalton walking down a forest trail in the direction of the castle.

Travelling in our compact group and shining our light beams across the leaf-and-twig littered floor, I could not help but make the resemblance to the island forest. A slight misty fog had only just begun to rise from the turf below. I felt safer in the large group armed with at least a few weapons but I was still growing a little anxious. Leaves rustled through the blackness of the trees, probably just wildlife. I knew this but yet I still worried.

"What kind of animals are out there? Anything to worry about?" I asked.

"Well Romania is home to over seventy percent of the brown bear population of Europe, but this is nothing to concern yourself about as they tend to stay clear of humans. Although I do not advise you to approach one with its young. That, my chum, would be a grave mistake," Dalton said.

"I see." I did not feel at all relieved by this insight.

It did not take long to find a clearing. Walking out onto the village street felt strange to me. All the buildings were completely different to those in England. None of them were just rectangular homes but were different shapes and sizes with brown and white wooden roofs and balconies. It seemed like a winter wonderland without a drop of snow in sight.

"I thought there'd be more gypsies," joked Bill.

There were no street lights, just the odd lantern hanging from a porch. I looked up and saw something I had never seen. The stars were shining without the effect of light pollution hiding them from sight. Not even the strange haze from the moon could block them out. I smiled and my anxious state left me. It was similar to the sights on the island but I was too preoccupied at the time to appreciate it.

Above the buildings I saw it. Bran Castle, towering over the village perched on its hill, its shadowy outline showing all sizes of walls and towers growing from the structure. The streets were peaceful and quiet with no one in sight. I was starting to like this place; it had a magical feel about it and was not what I had expected.

We entered a market place full of closed wooden stalls with small canopies, at the end of which was a small hut marking the entrance to the castle path closed off by a turnstile.

"Hope the royals are not home, it would be a rather unexpected visit," Dalton mentioned.

"Royals?" Jess asked.

"Mary and Ferdinand. I believe this castle belongs to them after the Romanian people revolted against their communist government. Holiday home when they wish, museum for the rest of the year," Dalton explained.

He really was just a fountain of knowledge this man, every little bit of history seemed to stick in his head. I know he probably had to research this place before our excursion but I had the feeling he was the type of gentleman that would find great pride in knowing everything just to show off.

"Well, I'm not paying to get in, I've never been one for castles," said Bill hopping over the turnstile.

We all followed over the gate and onto the castle premises. Little wooden huts were strewn all over the grounds, isolated from each other. A long path led up to the castle at the top of which stood a rocky structure supporting the straight and daunting castle walls, lifting high up as if birthed from the mountain rock itself.

The crunching of pebbles echoed under my step as we escalated the path.

"I suppose it's better than a hotel," Jess remarked with humour.

Reaching the top an eerie stone cross marked the summit, not any reassurance but no surprise everything was so gothic themed. To our left was a decline back down the other side of the hill and a little church stood out opposite a small street separated by a gently flowing river. To our right, the entrance to the castle, actually smaller than a normal door which was unexpected, was lit by a black lantern sticking from the wall. Worn writing was barely visible above the doorway. Small square wooden windows peered down, spying on what we were up to.

"So we just knock?" Bill asked.

"Guess again," retorted Dalton pulling a mall contraption from his jacket. He began fiddling with the lock until a click ushered the door to open.

"Voila!" Dalton stood to one side gesturing the way forward with a smirk.

Chapter 4

Anybody Home?

Silently making our way inside I gained my first glimpse of the castle's inner aesthetics. Dark wooden ceilings were a contrast to the bright white reworked walls and a small black gothic chandelier hung in the centre on some suspect-looking rope. It erupted into life as Bill flicked a nearby light switch. There were a few plaques and information boards hanging up on the walls for tourists to find out about its history.

Through a stone archway came a larger room. A small doorway was closed next to a set of narrow stairs and to the left was a large opening looking into the centre courtyard of the castle. The walls were set out in irregular fashion climbing to different heights, a main cylindrical tower rising above the rest complete with pointed cap. A walkway was present up high spanning all the way around the inside of the courtyard supported by wooden beams. Black metallic lanterns mounted on the wall lit the yard casting shadows over a small sign on the far wall indicating a gift shop.

Mounted high up on the wall inside was a life size portrait of a man dressed in rather eloquent attire of the olden days. Some form of black and red formal jacket with black trousers and a golden chain hanging from a pocket. A long sword was held in one hand with its tip balanced on the floor. He had slick black hair and a set of serious brown eyes, staring and judging those who looked at him.

"What a handsome chap," I joked. Underneath was an inscription in Romanian.

"Once a captive now a home," Dalton translated, although still too cryptic for me to understand.

Suddenly I realised my childlike curiosity had once again gotten the better of my brain as I peered at my wrist device. It was flashing the arrow wildly deeper into the castle. How stupid of me.

"Woah, wait!" I raised my arm. "There's one around somewhere!"

"It's never easy," Jess mentioned holding her pistol up so that her light allowed her to view the inner courtyard.

"This structure spans out in many different directions, our best option would be to split into two and head different ways to cover more ground," suggested Dalton.

"Split up?! It's not fucking Scooby Doo. It's not some man in a costume we're looking for! I'd rather be in a group if we find a Remnant." I objected to his ridiculous suggestion.

"Don't worry, Griff lad, I've seen this in films. It's usually the good looking one that dies so you've got nothing to worry about," Bill joked.

I was not amused. That was just plain hurtful, although something I would probably have said as well so, fair enough, I wouldn't want to be hypocritical and retaliate.

"Besides, you'll have Jess to take care of you. I'll watch Dalton's back, he looks like he needs my help." I frowned at him for a couple of seconds.

"No bother, let's go this way, Jess." I pointed to the right up some narrow wooden stairs.

"Watch you don't get yourself killed, you still owe me a pint," Bill concluded as he walked off across the central courtyard with Dalton, both with torches lighting the way.

Two people with weapons training have just left in the opposite direction and here I stand, a man of many traits yet all inappropriate to the situation, with Jess, a coastguard.

"Well, isn't this just dandy?"

"Will you stop your bitching and get up the stairs, Griff, you're starting to do my head in." Jess shoved me lightly in the back. Well that was quite harsh given the circumstances.

Marching upwards I slowly entered a room matching the aesthetics of the previous, the torch on my pistol beaming light through a large electric candle holder. Checking to my side I found another light switch and the candle holder turned on revealing old wooden furniture and paintings covering the walls.

Keeping my finger on the trigger I checked the next room. A large bed was to one side and a black wooden throne opposite with red material stitched on the backboard. Some mirrors and black-and-white photographs sat on the desk and bedside table. It was beginning to feel creepy. It didn't help it was so quiet; however I needed to be alert for any lurking Remnant. Silence is my friend I suppose.

"Pssst, Griff, this way," Jess whispered across the room.

"Griff? Jess? Found anything yet?" Bill's voice sounded over the comms device on my collar.

"No, not yet, just a load of creepy home design," I replied with the button held in on the little square radio.

"Alright, keep yourselves alert and ready for anything."

Jess led the way this time, going from room to room. It was hard to tell how many rooms we had been through as they were all the same: plain white walls, wooden floors and ceiling beams, eerie black iron light fittings, old paintings, black-and-white photos and old medieval-looking furniture.

Scenery changed slightly in one room as we entered through a large door up a mini set of steps. Through the door was a diagonal uneven stone stairway with an arched ceiling. Only a wobbly, worn rope anchored to one side gave support and one small light shining from halfway up the stairwell help with vision.

Reaching the top of the stairwell, Jess pushed the doorway open taking seemingly more force necessary than for a normal door. Entering I flashed the torch to all corners of the room to make sure it was clear before turning round and seeing that the door Jess had pushed was actually a bookshelf containing ancient looking literature.

"Secret passageway... Nice," I commented. It was pretty cool. I wondered how many more secret passageways were around, although my interest slowly waned and turned into worry when I realised if there were more passageways the Remnant could be using them to get behind us.

Through my sudden anxiety I shone the torch back down the stone stairwell just to double check we were not being snuck up on. Coast was clear.

I walked up to one of the windows overlooking the courtyard. The whole building was a mismatch of different sized walls and extrusions with the small courtyard in the middle giving a little escape to the mass amounts of stone and wood. Out of the corner of my eye I caught a glimpse of a shadow swiftly flash across an opposite window. I wasn't certain if I had actually seen anything as it was dark but it may have been something.

"Erm, Bill, Dalton. You aren't both next to a window right now?" I asked through the radio.

I waited a second for a reply.

"No, no we are just about to escalate some stairs," Dalton replied.

My concern grew. I saw their flashlights enter the room in which I had just seen the shadow, and Bill's face planted against the pane of glass looking back at me. A second later I swore I caught the shadow moving above them from another window.

"Guys, I think there is someone above you, I keep seeing shadows," I warned. Bills face turned from the window.

"Alright, Griff, we are going radio silent just in case, be very careful," Bill instructed.

The wrist device was still going crazy, pulsating like mad but remaining in the same position. If there was a Remnant moving around, the device was not detecting it, so if there was anyone at all it must be a human or possibly a possessed individual.

Moving into yet another room with Jess close behind I stopped still, a brief creaking sound echoed from the ceiling.

"What is it, Griff?" Jess whispered.

"Thought I heard someone above us," I whispered back. Jess nodded to go ahead.

This next corridor split into two directions, straight ahead into a room or up some stairs. Seeing as though I heard the sound from above and was feeling braver than usual with my company and weapon, I decided to take the stairs. I could not even see up them properly as they curved with the climb and on my way up I had to duck under a support beam – this castle was definitely not made for tall Englishmen.

There it was! A shadow floated across the room at the far end of the hallway. Without hesitation I left Jess on the curved stairs and sprinted toward the last room. It was dark and I tripped slightly and stumbled over the threshold. Instantly a bright light flashed into my eyes.

"Mr Holster what in God's name are you doing? I almost took your life away." The voice of Dalton came from behind the beam of light.

"Crap, I saw a shadow in this room but it must have been you."

"You saw a shadow that could have been a hostile and you ran straight into the room? Are you fucking stupid?" Bill scolded walking up from behind Dalton.

"You're right, I don't know why I did it. I got over excited I guess," I admitted.

"Being overzealous won't get you anywhere," Dalton commented.

Through my life I have never had a problem admitting when I was wrong. I knew the only way to learn would be from admitting to mistakes and being able to change my actions for future reference. In my eyes if you didn't admit to mistakes then you just increase your chances of making them again.

"Where's Jess, Griff?" asked Bill.

"She was right behind me." I turned back to peer down the long hallway. There was no sight of Jess. Maybe my hasty mistake would be more costly than I originally thought.

"Jess, Jess, where are you?" Bill enquired into the radio. We waited a couple of seconds. No reply.

"Ohh, you fucked up big time this time, Griff. She'd better be alright," Bill warned. Well now I felt like a disappointment. Deservedly so.

"No time to dilly dally. She could not have travelled far, and we must act swiftly." Dalton jogged forward down the hall.

Flying quickly down the stairs, Dalton and Bill instantly turned to the opposite direction I had come from toward a darkened end room. I arrived down the stairs with them both already entering and heard some kind of screeching shuffling noise from the room with the secret bookcase tunnel.

"Lads, I think I just heard something back there." I ushered to the two of them through the doorway.

"This room is clear anyway. Let's go," Bill commanded as he pushed past to take point again.

We burst into the room with the bookcase passage, torch beams spinning in all directions to ensure the room was clear. It was empty.

"I swear I heard something moving in this room."

"Are you sure? We need to keep looking. Jess might not even be in the castle anymore," Bill said getting worked up.

Dalton was too busy inspecting the grand piano set slightly off from the wall.

"Come on, lads, let's go, she's not in here," Bill instructed impatiently. Dalton continued to study the musical instrument and its surroundings.

"Dalton, would you get away from that thing!" Bill shouted across the room from the doorway.

"Do you not think it is a bit strange the bookshelves which encompass the room happen to leave a gap just behind the instrument?" he asked out of the blue.

"No, mate. I think your strange for thinking that when we have other stuff to worry about," Bill replied.

"Yeah, he's got a point, Dalton, Jess could be anywhere by now," I mentioned.

Despite us urging him to hurry, Dalton decided to take a seat. He placed his sidearm and metallic case on top of the piano and bent his head down to closer inspect the keys.

"Some of these keys are considerably more worn than the rest. I believe they are part of an old melody, Allegro Deciso by Béla Bartók, but that is just an educated guess with him being Romanian," he explained.

Before Bill could reply, Dalton began playing the melody of which he spoke of. It was only a few seconds in length but once completed the piano glided away from his hands with the eerie screeching noise I had heard from the other room, leaving a blackened hole in the ground.

"See, my friend, a bit of patience and thought gets you far, no need for such irrationality." Dalton smiled as he walked over to collect his equipment from the piano. Another secret passage, another possibility of a trap, a risk we would have to take to locate Jess. I had serious doubts about finding her there as I would have definitely heard the piano being played from so close, but it was still somewhere we had to check.

"Yeah, you are a bit of a hot head," I commented, backing up Dalton and trying to lighten the situation.

"I should just shoot you both and just fuck off back home."

I tried to find some humour in his annoyed expression.

Chapter 5

Lost and Found

Entering the spiral stone staircase we began our decent into the abyss in search of Jess. Flashing erratically the arrow on my wrist was warning of the Remnant threat nearby.

"I never heard any piano music upstairs. What makes you think Jess is down here?" I asked. "Also, on another note, my fancy gadget here is telling me there's a Remnant down here, so take care," I warned.

"That may be so, nevertheless it seems quite a mysterious passageway to just pass up. There could be clues to her disappearance. Besides, if Jess was indeed taken then locating the Remnant is our best chance of finding her, wouldn't you agree?" Dalton said.

Bill probably agreed but was stuck in a quiet mode of frustration trying to keep any thoughts to himself. Him being ex-military, I could only imagine the annoyance inside him at having to take orders from Dalton.

My weapon's beam of light showed millions of floating dust particles giving off a very ghostly vibe. I passed countless unlit wall-mounted oil lamps; God knows when they were last used. A shiver ran down my spine as the temperature began plummeting and my breath began to cloud the air. Checking behind to make sure I had not lost Dalton or Bill I was feeling increasingly unsure about the wisdom of walking down this strange passage.

Reaching the end a cold glow of blue light lit up the exit to the stairwell which was strange as I also started to hear the faint crackling noise of an open flame. Directly ahead was a large stone wall on which an enormous silhouette of a man was cast through an orange light.

"There's someone or something in there," I whispered. Both Dalton and Bill nodded and raised their weapons to eye level in unison.

As a tight group we marched through the stairwell archway ready to open fire if necessary. Within a couple of steps of leaving the relatively safe staircase I set foot on some form of pressure switch as the tiled stone floor slowly dipped downwards with a crunchy scraping noise.

"Aww, shit!" I exclaimed.

Bill was a second away from retreating back into the stairwell but was prevented by a set of steel bars that quickly erected themselves from the ground and slammed into the ceiling above. Before I knew it both directions were cut off by these large cylindrical columns. We were trapped.

Fine blue mist ran down the columns similar to that of the environmental suit I had worn on the island. We all faced the stairwell as Dalton pulled a pen from his jacket and tapped against one of the solid columns. On contact with the bar Dalton quickly retracted his hand as a thin crust of ice formed around the writing utensil holding it in place.

"Fascinating," whispered Dalton bending so that the pen was at eye level.

The same technology used to keep the Angious suit cold must be incorporated within this cell but it seemed like overkill to me. The bars were already arm thickness and I doubted anyone would be able to damage them.

"More unexpected guests I see," came a deep voice with a strange accent, which I could only assume was Romanian. Turning around I saw a tall figure poised behind the bars. Instantly I noticed the serious brown eyes I had seen on the portrait upstairs. Surely it could not be the same person? The painting was hundreds of years old. His whole get-up was exactly the same as depicted on the picture down to the long sword sheathed by his side. It had to be him.

Scanning the rest of the room there was a lot going on. The room itself was enormous, built and designed like a gothic cathedral hall but underground it had large arches with massive glass oil lamps hanging from the sides to light up the room with an orange glow. Large circular engraved pillars rose up to the ceiling to support the arches and, in the very centre of the room, was the machine we were searching for. Standing tall with its huge centre console and prism placed on the very top was the terraforming

Angious capsule. Four supporting crystal tubes were symmetrically placed in the corners of the room. At the opposite end of the room was what looked like an alter with a flat stonewall surrounded by another cage built from the same cylindrical bars which currently kept us prisoner. Suspended from the ceiling was a large metallic cylinder angled down from the capsule's glass prism down into the cage at the far wall. Three small doors lined up on each side of the room underneath a large black cable, which led from the centre console across both sides of the hall. The doors were wooden and matched the theme of the room apart from the furthest left door, which gleamed from a metallic coating. Next to the centre console were some extra machines, which looked ancient compared to modern technology. It had large levers and dials everywhere like something you would find in an old Frankenstein movie. These machines were accompanied by large wooden tables littered with glass vials filled with various liquids. A wooden rack next to the tables contained an assortment of sharpened weapons that gleamed in the orange light.

Bill raised his rifle aiming directly at the man's face with every intention of pulling the trigger.

"I don't know who you are but the next move you make had better be letting us out of this cell," Bill asserted.

The man smirked.

"Sir, I do not believe you are in a position to be telling me what to do."

"I'd say I'm in the perfect position to blow your brains out, pal," Bill threatened.

"Try it at your leisure, sir, you would be wasting your time," the man taunted.

BANG!

Catching me by surprise I was almost deafened by the sound of Bill's rifle firing. Even more surprisingly the man's head had not been blown into a million pieces but instead the bullet had been frozen at such an extreme speed that it had frozen in place just ahead of the two bars, the tip aiming directly at the man's forehead.

"For fuck's sake!" yelled Bill in a small tantrum, slamming his rifle down to the ground and causing it to clatter on the floor.

"Projectiles are prevented from entering or exiting the freezing barrier," the man explained standing calmly with his hands behind his back.

"Yeah, but I bet it won't stop this." I held my arm up with my fist clenched, and aimed it directly toward his chest. The luminous orange crosshairs appeared, guiding my weapon. The man's eyes widened slightly as he removed his arms from behind his back and pointed toward my wrist.

"Where did you acquire that device?" he asked in a surprised manner.

"Not so big now are you, pretty boy? So how about letting us out 'cause I have a feeling you and I both know what will happen if I set this bad boy off in your chest." I felt like I had just gained an upper hand on the situation.

"Just tell me where you found the device and I may let you free," the man replied.

"An Angious called Zarathus gave it to me," I answered.

His posture changed from a static commanding position to that of an excited school child as he hurried over to the wall where he continued to pull on a large wooden lever.

"You know of Zarathus! There is a name I have not heard in a long time. You must tell me what has become of him," he asked excitedly as the bars began to lower from the ceiling.

Bill was ready to hurdle the bars before Dalton grabbed his arm and prevented him from launching an attack in his enraged state.

"I don't believe hurting this man will solve anything." Dalton attempted to calm Bill down.

"Please, what of Zarathus?" the man asked once more walking over to me and staring searchingly for the answer he desired.

"He's gone. He possessed a good friend of mine and died saving us from an Angious called Lucifer."

His face instantly dropped at this revelation.

"Oh, no. He always did what was necessary. That is a shame… But Lucifer, he is dead, correct?"

"The last we saw of them both they were in the depths of the sea and were caught up in the blast of one of those things going off." Bill pointed to the capsule device behind the man.

"You know of a method of destroying the device? This is excellent, you must share this information."

By this time the columns had fully vanished into the stone floor, the pen and bullet both lay on the ground still covered in a layer of white frost.

"Excuse me, but perhaps you could answer us a few questions yourself. In particular, have you seen a young woman of a small height with blonde hair roaming around?" queried Dalton.

The man turned himself back around to face us as we all gathered around him.

"Ahh but of course, I apologise. She is a friend of yours then, yes?" He walked over to one of the old wooden side doors. "I had spotted the intruder upstairs but I had not realised she had company!" he explained.

There was something extremely odd about him that I could not put my finger on – I mean, apart from the fact he almost perfectly resembled the portrait I had seen upstairs which happened to be ancient. The way his attitude seemed to change almost spontaneously from serious to carefree was worrying. Aside from this I was pretty glad we had found the capsule with relative ease as well as finding the location of Jess. Everything was going slightly more smoothly than expected.

Bang! Bang!

Flinching from the sudden burst of fire, I turned to see Bill had fired a couple of rounds at the capsule but to no avail. My heart almost skipped a beat.

"What in God's name do you think you are doing?!" Dalton raised his voice for the first time since meeting him.

"Don't you fucking shout at me, mate! We are here to blow this thing up so that's what I'm trying to do!" Bill yelled back, getting right up in Dalton's face.

The man joined the group looking concerned to the nature of this argument and pushed the two men apart.

"The capsule creates gravitational energy and is protected by a shield of gravity. Any impacts from space debris cannot cause the device harm, your weapons, and even the wrist device will do nothing. You have too much anger.

"Were it so easy I'd have done it myself, but no, the entire console is joined together with metal plating which can be manipulated using electrical current. Basically, you put the panels in place, add a current and the panels fold into shape creating a perfect seal, much like the device on your arm," he described, pointing at my wrist.

"The only way you are getting rid of this thing is with Angious tools which I'm afraid are not an option. I created makeshift machinery with your primitive technology to harness just a small amount of the device's power but the only option we have to destroy this thing is overloading the gravity field.

"Its main power source is fusion batteries designed to last millennia. I managed to reverse the polarity of one of the batteries meaning instead of giving energy it takes it in the form of thermal energy. I connected the cable to the outer shell without compromising the device which now draws out all heat from the cable and anything attached," he continued before exiting the group and walking through the wooden door without a second glance back.

"Nothing is ever easy is it?" Bill said walking past me as he tried to calm down, his face red with frustration.

Following the strange man through to the next room I realised that once again I was acting on blind obedience. I should really start questioning my actions sooner. For all I know it's another trap waiting for me, and here I am, the wandering fly heading for the web.

Luckily entering the room there was no trap waiting for us, instead Jess sat in the centre tied to an old wooden chair.

"Well it's about time you all showed up. This weirdo wouldn't believe anything I said and that asshole over there won't shut his mouth either." Jess nodded her head to one side.

"My most sincere apologies, you must understand, there are certain precautions one must undertake," the strange man said.

At the back of the stone room were two more cages built from the freezing columns. A man resided inside one of them, tall, long blond hair and a small beard. Quite young looking, he was sat on a stool facing us.

"More company for me? How delightful," the imprisoned man commented with a sadistic smile.

"Shut your mouth, Lucian," commanded the strange man as he untied Jess.

Jess ran over and embraced me. She was freezing to the touch.

"Aw, well, isn't that lovely?" mocked Lucian from his prison.

"Do not force my hand, Lucian. I will take you to the chamber," the strange man threatened. I had no clue what the chamber was or what was in it but it seemed shut this Lucian character up for a brief moment.

We began exiting the room back into the main hall.

"You can't leave now. We were just getting to know one ano–" The door was closed before Lucian could finish.

"Alright. Time for some answers, I think. Who the hell are you? Who the hell is that in there? And where the hell is the Remnant?" I asked the barrage of questions looking at my wrist device which was flashing the red arrow to the opposite side of the room to the furthest door away.

The man continued to the middle door opposite.

"All of your questions will be answered shortly. Please, enter and take a seat." He held the wooden door open.

Notably the first big difference when entering this new room was the temperature. I did not feel as if I was trekking the North Pole anymore. Red and orange flames danced at a fireplace in the wall surrounded by a group of old couches and seats – this was the crackling sound I heard earlier. Above the fireplace was an exotic wall-mount of crossed swords. This must be his social room, although I doubt it had been used much as only one of the seats was free from dust.

Blowing the cobwebs from one of the red leather seats I took my place alongside the rest of the group. We all sat staring in an awkward silence.

"Well?" Bill broke the silence.

The strange man hesitated for a second.

"My name... is Dracula."

Chapter 6

The Legend

This is slightly surreal. First angels and demons are kind of real, and now one of the most famous characters in horror history is real. Or maybe he is pulling my leg and he is actually someone else. Or maybe it is all just a big coincidence. He can't be *the* Dracula, that's insane – although insanity seems to be a running theme in my life at the moment. I'm probably dead, that's it. There was no island and none of this crazy stuff is real. I'm just dead and this is what happens when you die, you get sent to one big crazy dream world.

"Oww!" I exclaimed as Jess punched my arm. I had become lost in my thoughts and was staring open mouthed like an idiot. It was not one of my most impressive moments.

"No way," I announced eventually.

"Yes, it is true. I am Dracula, but also Ophanim. You may call me one or the other it makes no difference as we are now one."

"Ophanim?" Dalton enquired listening in with utmost interest.

"Correct. I was Ophanim, an Angious guard sent on the same mission as Zarathus but to another location on Helvius. I must have made it through the portal before Zarathus and ended up here a long, long time ago. I bonded with a prisoner here, Dracula it turned out to be, who had quite a reputation amongst the villagers. Anyway we escaped the prison and from there on we built this castle protecting the device and preventing further use of the portal. We have been together for so long that neither of us seeks control over the body, instead we share it as one."

I continued to stare in amazement. It *was* the count from the portrait. I knew it!

"Please allow me to introduce our small faction. Here we have Bill Greaves, Jessica Hart, Griffin Holster and myself, Dalton Meier," Dalton presented. It struck me that I never actually acquired Bill's surname. Slightly embarrassing on my behalf as I probably should have asked by now.

"So, you're not a vampire then?" asked Bill out of the blue.

"Vampire. Ha-ha. That was a tale the locals came up with a while ago. Of course some Remnant had escaped through the portal before me and had possessed some of the villagers. The only way I could make sure they were finished was with a stake through the heart or the removal of the head, although the whole neck-biting thing was an extra, which sort of stuck. I would go out at night and try to eliminate these Remnant, but it was too difficult to differentiate between who was possessed and who was not to rid this place of them all. I allowed the vampire tale to remain to keep the villagers from entering the castle and discovering the device. Lucian in the other room is possessed by a Remnant and decided to pay me a visit. I am still working on a way to find out who has been possessed, using Lucian for my experiments, but with your device I may be able to finally complete my work!"

At this point even Dalton seemed a little dumbfounded.

"How do you know none of us are possessed then? You acted pretty fast to let us all free?" I asked intrigued.

"Intuition and experience. I have seen centuries of Remnant possession, but there are still only a few that elude me. Although your gravitational distorter device was a big giveaway, only the elite of our special forces would carry them," he explained.

"So what became of your device if you don't mind me asking?" interrupted Dalton.

"It just so happens that when exiting the portal I was not alone. I fended myself from many Remnant. All of my equipment was destroyed and I was on the edge of death when I bonded to Dracula who, in turn, saved me. Without any means of returning through the portal I had to adapt to this world, preventing any further portal use."

"You've been alive all this time, living alone down here. That must be horrible!" asked a concerned Jess.

Ophanim stood up and walked over to the open flame.

"I was not always alone. There have been friends in the past, even a woman; but time does not bode well for those of this domain. Countless lives have been surpassed by my own, too many to endure any longer. I have but one remaining contact; Andrei, a villager who works for me by keeping the castle in check, purchasing supplies for myself. We never meet in person and he has no idea of what resides here. Being alone brings less heartache."

More silence passed as his head dipped in front of the flames. I could never imagine the pain of seeing centuries of loved ones being taken away from me. It must be truly terrible. I suppose having a lengthened lifespan could be seen as a curse when everyone around you does not possess the same ability. Even Bill who seemed to have calmed from his angered state was quiet and withheld any comment, possibly having the same thoughts.

"So all this time all you have done is work on how to find the possessed Remnant?" asked Jess.

"Most of my time, yes. Although I also perfected my swordsmanship and took the time to learn about this world, its inhabitants, the languages."

"Yeah, I was starting to wonder how your English was so good," announced Jess.

"If you taught yourself everything then why is this place so old fashioned? And what if some possessed comes at you with a gun? I don't care how good you are throwing a big knife around, a bullet to the head is game over," enquired Bill.

"Well, to answer one question at a time. Being old fashioned just gives me a homely feel from when I first arrived, being here for such a long time I like to retain my memories, plus I do not like to leave the device for long periods of time. As for your second comment, the Remnant do not wish to stand out, a gun would ring alarm bells for the rest of the villagers and if one did come for me at night I have the advantage of stealth and narrow hallways in my castle," Ophanim explained.

Sliding round on his heels, Ophanim turned to face us with a forced smile and open arms.

"But now that you are all here I can finally complete my life's work!" he exclaimed with a burst of life.

"Alright, that's all well and good but my device here is still telling me there's a Remnant down here, so maybe you'll want to get rid of it first yeah?" I suggested tapping the shell of the wrist device, which was pointing the red arrow to the room sealed by the metallic door.

"There is no need to worry. I was capable of capturing one of the creatures. It is being held in the next room in the cryocell, as I like to name it." Ophanim explained.

"This cryocell... the very same we clumsily triggered on entry to your... well, lair?" enquired Dalton.

"Correct. Remnant are rendered blind when surrounded by low temperatures, they cannot withstand the cold. By syphoning energy from the terraforming device I can create the freeze around the cell. It is extremely effective," he explained.

"Quite ingenious," complimented Dalton.

"Well you learn a lot in a century or two," joked Ophanim in better spirits.

"If it pleases you all I would rather like it if Griffin accompanies me to the capsule. You may all join or remain in this relatively comfortable room. It is your choice," Ophanim said walking toward the door.

Seems I didn't get much of a choice in the matter.

"There's something a little off about him. I don't care if he's not a vampire or if he's one of those angel blokes, I think we should watch ourselves around him," whispered Bill leaning over in his seat.

My rule has always been to give everyone a chance to prove they are trustworthy until proven otherwise, it's just in my good nature, some may call it naivety but I could still see where Bill was coming from.

Rising from the brief comfort of my antique chair I patted any excess dust from my trousers and exited the warm living area back into the frosty main hall with its gothic undertone.

"What do you reckon, Dalton? Should I do what this person wants?" I asked for a second opinion.

"It would be wonderful to finally see one of these machines functioning. Also if what he plans to do actually works then we may have the tool necessary to finally eradicate the Remnant from our time for good. So my advice would be to go along for the ride," answered Dalton.

I didn't really appreciate his answer. Perhaps I would have liked him to show at least some concern such as Bill did but, at the end of the day, he had come here to do a job.

"How come your gang haven't found a way to see if someone is possessed yet? You've all been around for a while as well," I asked.

"Oh there have always been ways to tell, Mr Holster, except every method so far requires the capture of the test subject. Even since the old times we had the so-called witch trials, very primitive ways of discovering if someone was possessed; very successful apart from the hundreds of innocents who were drowned or burned alive. We tend to stay away from that variety of testing nowadays."

"Oh, well, nothing wrong with a good ol' friendly burning at the stake, get some drinks, get the lads around, set a fire…." I said with complete sarcasm. Dalton did not appreciate my sense of humour and I cringed as he turned away.

Ophanim was waiting patiently by the main console of the large device, the perfectly rounded crystal orb with its tiny extruding spikes set within the panel. Just above was the crystal tube with the same swirling blue dot I remembered from when Zarathus programmed the self-destruct sequence for my wrist device.

"Everything is set in motion my friend, Griff. Please place your hand on the orb and begin."

Chapter 7

Armageddon

The group had gathered behind me waiting in anticipation as I stood in front of the control orb.

"Well, here we go again," I announced before slowly and carefully placing the palm of my hand onto the control orb. Pain was instantly numbed as the tiny spikes connected with my nervous system. Connecting up to the system I began seeing various screens encompassing the room, all of which were in a language I could not comprehend. A download bar appeared on the main screen directly across the console exactly like it had back on the island. Instinctively I gazed down to watch as the golden glow of the data transfer raced across my hand like a million tiny ants up into the wrist device.

"Is it working?" Jess asked.

It did not take long for the download bar to fill and the golden stream to vanish out of sight. Removing my hand from the orb looked worse than it actually was as the needles left the skin without leaving any trace of their entry.

"Well it's done something," I answered turning to face the group.

Taking a couple of steps toward Lucian's room I checked my wrist device. Disappointingly the arrow was still pointing behind me to the room where the Remnant was being contained.

"Well that's a let-down," I commented.

"I'm assuming it was unsuccessful. Back to the drawing board it is, Mr Ophanim?" suggested Dalton.

"I was worried this may occur. I believe I can rectify this by obtaining a control orb from my time. The data from this console is ancient and corrupted," Ophanim explained.

"And there's no way for us to get through the portal without one of those suits you had on last time, Griff, is there?" Jess asked looking at me. I don't know why she was asking me. I travelled through the portal once, it didn't make me the expert on time travel and alien environments.

"I honestly don't know how to answer that, Jess."

"No, but perhaps I can help with this little dilemma," grinned Dalton patting the large metal case he had been lugging around the entire time. "If you would be so kind as to produce one of these gateways I believe I can retrieve the orb for you," he added.

"Please explain yourself," Ophanim said, looking confused.

"It would be simpler if I just showed you," answered Dalton placing the metallic case on one of the wooden tables.

Opening the dual latches the case lid popped upwards automatically positioning itself perpendicular to the bottom half. Centred in the case was a small football-sized metallic sphere which was segmented into numerous silvery overlapping blades. Either side of the ball were thin square glass screens. On removing the ball from the case I could see that it was attached by a long extremely fine cable on some form of reel and also that the bottom of the ball had a flat surface. As soon as the ball was removed the screens were lifted upwards out of the case. The left screen had another screen hidden behind it which rotated to the top position, the right screen also had an extra screen which rotated to the bottom position so that there were four screens in all four compass points. A small controller popped out of the bottom of the case onto the old wooden table.

"Let us see if this works," said Dalton. He rolled the ball along the stone floor. It bobbled across the uneven surface pulling the tether behind it until it came to a rest on the flat bottom about ten meters away from the group. Picking up the controller he began pressing some random buttons. The screens from the case behind us kicked into life showing a light green glow like some form of night vision. Just seconds later the ball began moving, the segments spun downwards and outwards into a metallic rose shape. Within the rose was a square machine that looked to have a fan on each side face. The machine began unfolding so that all four fans were facing upwards and burst into life lifting up the small undercarriage into the air free from the ball. Four small cameras and a small metallic ring made up the undercarriage. Dalton played with the controller as the machine flew toward us with little to no sound. I turned to look at the screens to find a panoramic view of the room which was no longer in the night vision mode.

"That is extremely awesome," gasped Jess in amazement. It was pretty damn cool, I had to agree.

"This is a prototype surveyor drone developed to be used through the portal to survive the harsh conditions on the other side without having personnel enter. The theory is that the stainless steel ball protects the drone from the black goop of the portal, which also opens up into the antenna array wired back to our side of the portal. The drone shall give us full vision of the other side. The ring on the bottom can be magnetised which could allow it to retrieve the orb, although initially it was designed for any artefacts we could locate. I hope it will function in this manner at any rate; we have never tried it ourselves as opening a portal has always been deemed too dangerous," explained Dalton flying the drone to the control panel on the capsule device.

Hovering just above the control orb the disc below the drone began glowing red. Below the drone the orb began to vibrate and then suddenly shot up onto the drone with a clean *ting* sound. Dalton smiled at his own excellent manoeuvring skills, clearly loving his new toy.

Ophanim inspected the screens closely. "I am liking this idea. I can open a portal for us. It may still be dangerous but it must be done."

Well at least I wouldn't have to venture through that dreaded gateway to Helvius again. What a nightmare that had turned out to be the first time.

Dalton dropped the orb back onto the console and proceeded to fly the drone back into the antenna where it folded up and curled back into a ball.

Ophanim led us behind the capsule to the far wall. Two large levers were set next to the cage. Pulling the first lever caused a few of the columns to retreat into the floor with a loud screech which echoed around the hall.

"I hope you are all prepared, there could be countless Remnant waiting to traverse the gateway… Or maybe we will get lucky you just never know," Ophanim warned.

Everyone took hold of their individual weapons in preparation. Upon pulling the second lever a hatch opened up in the ceiling above the capsule. Natural light from the moon shone through onto the prism which then transferred the time signal through the tube and into the cage.

"The tube is like a, how is it said... fibre optic, full of mirrors to send the time code through the bars uninterrupted," explained Ophanim.

The signal met the double circle which was standing up in the centre of the cage. Before I knew it the black tar-like substance began forming across the wall like an eerie ectoplasm until the gateway was once again open in front of me. The path to hell awaited.

Dalton removed the ball from the package. Jess, Bill and Ophanim took up positions around the portal as I remained standing guard next to Dalton.

"Let us see if the workers back at the lab are worth what we pay them," announced Dalton as he threw the ball through the portal which sucked up the tether from the case like a metallic string of spaghetti.

All four screens from the case burst into life as Dalton started up the drone. I waited in eager anticipation. Then there was light. It had made it – there was a three-sixty view of the surroundings through the portal. Currently all there was to see was the antenna array on one side and another control console on the other. The room was lit with an orange glow of light.

Moving a joystick the drone rose up from the array to fully view the area. Now in full view of the portal I could see what can only be described as a lava fall directly behind the gateway causing the orange glow. Noticeably the portal was a great deal larger than the last one I had encountered, almost the size of a normal detached house. Console and equipment were strewn across the room exactly as I'd seen before; the only things missing were the lava tubes and the monstrous statue of the Remnant. Over next to the large cavern entrance was the panel containing the control orb. Dalton skilfully flew the drone toward it.

"Where are all the Remnant? I would have thought they would all be trying to get through while they can," I asked confused. It was strange that they were nowhere to be seen. Because of the empty nature of the room, the rest of the group let down their guard and joined to watch the screens in the case.

"I was just wondering the same thing," replied Dalton.

Flying the drone to the orb the screen began to shake giving off a loud rumbling noise through the speakers as if it had been hit by some sort of shockwave.

"Woah! Is that supposed to happen?" asked Bill.

"It most certainly is not, Mr Greaves," replied Dalton with concentration on his face.

Dalton continued and attempted to lower the drone to the orb before the screen shook violently once more. Then from the screen showing the tunnel entrance was a bright green flash, followed by another, and another until they were occurring every couple of seconds. The rumbling continued showering dust across the room.

"What is going on out there?" mumbled Dalton to himself.

Giving in to curiosity and the annoyance of being disrupted on his mission, Dalton directed the drone to the exit of the cave to find out what exactly was causing the tremors and flashing lights.

When the drone finally reached the exit I stood in awe, mouth wide open at the chaotic scene which was unfolding on Helvius – it was total war.

Once again the portal laboratory was situated within an active volcano. Black clouds of toxic gasses spewed into the atmosphere raining down a barrage of fire and rock. The black and yellow desert land was stretched for miles ahead with a river of volcanic material running down the side of the volcano. Near the bottom, where the river ended, was a gigantic portion of the gravity disc at least thirty storeys high, strewn across a large crater, slowly being melted from the superheated pool of lava. The main bulk of the wreckage was situated further off in the distance.

Up in the sky loomed the bright blue pearl which was Hesthenon shining onto Helvius like a dim second sun. It was clear that the two planets were still a great distance apart but being so massive it seemed closer than it actually was, it was all a matter of perspective. It would still take a long time for the planets to collide but the difference in the portal time could mean that it would take centuries back in my time. It all depended on how long and regularly the portals remained open on Earth's side. If the portals remained constantly open on Earth then the time difference would be zero.

Yet amongst this amazing scenery of alien worlds was a swarm of Remnant beasts both on foot and in the sky circling the wreckage and Angious armies.

The drone flew to a higher position closer to the action. On the opposite side of the wreckage were shuttle craft dropping off thousands of Angious soldiers who were fighting off wave after wave of Remnant attempting to gain control of the higher ground on top of the disc wreckage.

Streams of green lights lit up the battlefield mowing down the persistent Remnant monsters. Clouds of blue Remnant blood rose into the sky as it evaporated in the heat of the planet's harsh environment, whilst Angious were being torn to bits without hesitation. Remnant bellowed their horrific roar as Angious soldiers screamed in pain as they were obliterated by the Remnants' claws and teeth. Green flashes flew by in the sky as the few Angious who managed to reach the summit of the wreckage were engaged by the flying hordes. One soldier was plucked from the top and dropped from the side cascading down into the lava pool below – it was horrifying.

An elongated shuttle made a swoop over the Remnant side of the disc wreckage dropping fist-sized balls all around the Remnant, they hovered a few feet above the ground before crumpling in on themselves dragging any nearby Remnant into the gravity field causing their bodies to mash into one another until the balls finally exploded spewing out a final blue mist; almost like an Angious gravity version of a cluster bomb. Another shuttle tried to make a similar run until a flying Remnant slammed into its side, forcing the vehicle to collide into the side of the wreckage causing a large explosion collapsing a section of the structure to further rubble.

"Holy shit, what is going on?" exclaimed Bill.

"It seems it has become public knowledge about the portals. This is what we feared may happen and what we aimed to prevent. This time does not belong to the Remnant or the Angious but many are not willing to face the sacrifice we chose for our people," explained Ophanim. "Oh no..." he continued, "it's Malphas." It was the first time I had seen any Angious or Remnant in a real state of fear.

Glancing back at the screen I saw his cause for concern. Standing tall at the rear of the Remnant swarms was a large beastly Remnant at least four times the size of the ones already faced. One of the cameras zoomed in closer and I realised the monster leading the army was the same as the beastly stone statue I had seen in the previous portal laboratory. It had two large horns extruding from its skull, its arms and claws easily the size of a human's. The most terrifying was the necklace of Angious skulls around its neck which met with hundreds of scars around its scaly black and red skin. It certainly looked like the type of thing you would fear – the stuff of nightmares.

The drone shook once more as another shockwave unbalanced the air. On the Angious side of the wreckage was the source of the disturbance. Three large shinning chrome tank-like vehicles were aiming into the wreckage where the lava did not reach. Hovering above the ground with a green neon glow, underneath they were mounted with large twin cannons. Orange rings began to glow up along the long nozzles, one by one spinning orange until the cannons fired in unison. The two red beams converged into one large stream which hammered into the side of the wreckage and, within seconds of the impact, the air imploded causing wreckage to fly in all directions and cutting Remnant into small pieces. Smaller mounted weapons tore up the remaining Remnant attempting to approach the tank turning them into copious amounts of Swiss cheese.

"What's with the light show? My device doesn't turn any colour," I asked inquisitively.

"It all has to do with the time and energy of the device. These weapons work on the same principle as a black hole except on a much smaller scale. Black holes are the densest gravitational anomalies in existence and reflect and emit no light, but if we harness that power we can create directional gravitational changes with different densities. Your wrist device is relatively very weak and does not refract any light. The rifle, however, has a longer range because the burst of gravity lasts a longer length of time which emits the green light. The Goliath tank is a prototype which we thought may be too dangerous as the time and energy input was so unstable we didn't know what the outcome might be. Turns out the red beam must be closest to black hole energy, they have taken a large risk using these tanks but it seems they are willing to do anything to survive," explained Ophanim.

Suddenly looking back at the screen the left tank was just about to fire its main cannons, until suddenly the rear end dipped causing the beam to fire wildly upwards to the upper portion of the wreckage at its own people, tearing them in half and then blasting the remains over the sides of the structure. Almost completely upright the tank was pulled down into the sand by some sort of blue-shelled tentacles until within seconds it was gone from sight. This was insane. Even after all I had been through I had never witnessed such brutality; limbs thrown about, lifeless bodies everywhere. It was obvious that capturing the portal was the only option for the Angious, as more and more were dropped off from the shuttle craft.

Continuing the assault on the wreckage the remaining two tanks fired shots which rippled through the air, contorting flesh and metal alike as it demolished section by section of the disc. The opposite side of the wreckage began to show weakness as small parts flew away from the beam implosion. Two fully chrome-armoured Angious soldiers defending the right tank were mowed down by a group of Remnant, screaming as they were dismembered. Overwhelmed by sheer numbers even the tank's weapons could not cope. Before long the tentacles appeared again yanking the vehicle into the sand dunes.

"It's a God damn massacre," I said without taking my eyes off the screen. I was so focused I don't think I blinked for the entirety of the fight.

"This is terrible! Do we have to watch this? It's horrible," said Jess sickened.

Lucky enough not to have lived in a time when war was ripe, I was more than astounded at the ferocity at which both sides fought. Watching from a neutral perspective I knew I didn't want either side to win as it would mean them eventually making their way through the portal to our time. Be it viscous monsters or heavily armed humanoids, both wanted to take our time from us. Obviously having the Angious victorious would be more favourable, but what would happen if the number of people willing to be possessed were less than the number of Angious entering our time? In front of me showed a race of people willing to go through any amount of extremes to survive and that would surely also mean possessing people against their will. We could not let that happen.

Another shuttle arrived closer to the battlefield right behind the remaining tank dropping off only three personnel. Two of them wore extra gold and chrome exoskeleton armour to carry heavier gear. Armed with larger weapons when fired they produced a stream of white frost which turned any Remnant in the vicinity to lifeless statues.

Forming two frosty barricades the two soldiers prevented any normal humanoid Remnant from attacking the tanks. The Angious in the centre was taller than the rest and had red stripes across his armour as well as black metallic spikes across his arms and legs with two chrome razor-like horns on his futuristic helmet which was tinted to hide his face. His armour looked almost like the lovechild of a tank and a Remnant. His weapon of choice was not the usual gravity device used by his allies but some form of sword. Grasping the black and red handle with both hands a chrome shaft ran upwards almost ten feet in height. It was a beast of a weapon. From its base just above the handle, three nozzles span around the shaft causing a heat wave kind of aura to emit all the way to the tip creating the effect of a ghostly lance.

"Vaniah, he commands the Angious fleet. My God, they have sent everything," Ophanim said.

Vaniah marched past his two soldiers toward the remaining tank. Two of the lingering Remnant lashed toward him but with two swift movements he cut them down in their stride spraying blue blood into the air that instantly misted up in a cloudy vapour. He took no time to admire his handiwork. Reaching the tank he mounted the vehicle dicing up the blue-shelled tentacles that rose to meet him. Diving back down to the floor he stabbed wildly before punching down into the ground and dragging out the carcase of an oversized scorpion monster with tentacles instead of pincers and missing a large rear stinger. It was at least twice the size of Vaniah but that did not stop him hurling the body to one side.

Attempting to climb back aboard the remaining tank, Vaniah was met by the talons of an overzealous flying Remnant. Clawing at his body the Remnant was dragged to the floor by Vaniah. Using his ghostly lance he dispatched one of the Remnant's wings causing it to writhe in pain and lash out wildly. Timing his move perfectly, Vaniah dodged the crazed lunges and dove into the Remnant thrusting the lance into its abdomen. He sliced upward holding onto the Remnant's head until it parted from its body in a burst of blue mist.

Throwing the severed head of the beast to the ground he marched back over to the tank which had just fully charged another shot. By this time hundreds of Angious had gathered up behind him encouraged by his momentum and excellence on the battlefield.

Red lights burst from the tank's primary cannons as it destroyed the final section of the wreckage. Through the newly formed hole, a mass swarm of Remnant rushed onto the Angious side of the disc.

Mounted firmly on the remaining tank Vaniah pointed toward the opening with his lance and screamed something in the Angious language. Boosting forwards the tank hovered toward the hole, mowing down the waves of Remnant, its cannons started to charge as it entered the disc. A lengthy red beam erupted from the wreckage obliterating a line of Remnant and creating a path for the tank to enter. Streams of Angious followed the tank through the hole over the only patch of land untouched by the lava pool as Vaniah chopped down any approaching Remnant. The Angious leader bellowed as loud as he could as the following Angious soldiers yelled out in unison as they followed their commander.

Snipers had managed to win over the top of the wreckage using the first rail gun type weapon I had seen used. Every shot they took completely obliterated any Remnant in a beam of concentrated energy.

It seemed like the Remnant were finally on the back foot. Completely oblivious to anything other than the battle, it had taken too long to realise Malphas had noticed the strange flying drone above the warzone. He pointed toward it with a terrifying roar.

"Oh dear, I think it may be time to go," announced Dalton steering the drone back toward the cave entrance.

Before entering the cave the rear camera picked up the final scene of Malphas charging at the tank tearing his giant claw straight through its hull. Vaniah flew over the top landing back first onto the ground. The pair of them began fighting amongst the green lightshow and massacre of creatures.

Remnant could be seen climbing the side of the volcano as the drone finally entered the cave for good.

"Shit! You'd better hurry Dalton, those bastards are right behind you," Bill said.

"Yes, I am well aware of the situation, Mr Greaves," answered Dalton feeling the pressure.

With little time to spare, Dalton lowered onto the console and latched on to the crystal orb. He then flew as smoothly as possible over to the antenna array and dropped down into the centre. The last video footage from the drone was two Remnant entering the cave.

"Fucking hell, watch the portal!" I yelled in panic as the tether began reeling in the antenna ball.

The ball flew through the portal covered in the black goop and was followed by two overly angered Remnant monsters covered in a thick layer of the tar-like substance. I managed to dive out of the cage followed by the rest of my companions. Dalton had managed to swipe the case pulling the antenna through behind him. Ophanim smashed his arms against the levers on the wall in a hurry to close the portal and the cage.

One of the Remnant creatures managed to escape the bars closing on the cage but Ophanim was ready with his sword and cut the beast diagonally across the chest in one swoop. It dropped to the floor in two parts before phasing out of existence.

The second Remnant attempted to lunge in our direction. Unable to see us through the cold wall it thrust its arm through the bars causing it to freeze solid. Screeching, it tried to withdraw completely detaching itself from its forearm. Ophanim switched the lever back opening the cage with a metallic screech.

"What are you doing?" enquired Jess, confused.

Without answering, Ophanim walked casually toward the flailing demon and calmly pushed his sword into its chest.

Chapter 8

The Possessed

The situation on Hesthenon and Helvius was dire. It was carnage, complete and utter desperation at its maximum. Was I surprised – probably not. I've seen fanatical people fighting for what they believe in on the news, fighting for survival. To see an entire race fighting so ferociously for survival was not a surprise but it was nevertheless brutal. No mercy was shown between the two sides, no real strategy to the fight. It was chaos, reminiscent of no-man's-land from the First World War. It had become clearer now than ever before that the portals had to somehow be shut down for good.

Ophanim exited the cage sheathing his sword.

"Feral and lacking intelligence, what a waste of a soul" uttered Ophanim depressed at seeing his people slaughtered.

"I believe this is what you wished for," said Dalton throwing the orb over to Ophanim.

"Indeed, it seems your little device was a worthy acquisition. Now it is my turn to prove myself," commented Ophanim swapping the orbs from the control panel of the capsule device.

Placing his hand on the spiked side of the orb, Ophanim began smiling.

"The control panel is recognising the oddities in the orb. Extracting this information I can use it so that your wrist device can detect any energy caused by time abnormalities in the area and not just the Remnant signature," he explained. "If you would kindly place your hand back on the orb I believe this time will be more successful."

"Well, here we go again then," I said as I pushed my hand against the spiked orb.

Tiny injections connected me to the console and again began transferring the data to my wrist device.

"You know, I'm getting a bit sick of doing all the real work around here. You're all welcome to chip in at any time," I joked trying to lighten the mood.

"Well, we can always take your arm off and I'll happily give the device a go," Bill kidded straight-faced. Or at least I hoped he was kidding, I could never tell sometimes.

"Ha-ha, nice one." I gave a nervous laugh pointing toward Bill with my free hand. His facial expression did not change.

"O…K," I whispered to myself turning back to the console to find the transfer was complete.

"How are we fairing, Mr Holster? Cooking on gas?" probed Dalton.

Removing my hand from the orb the arrow instantly moved around to point toward the door containing Lucian. The arrow above the device swapped direction between the captured Remnant to Lucian's room as I moved back and forth. I couldn't help a large grin crossing my face as I looked at the group.

"We're cooking all right," I commented.

"It's pointing at both the remnant and Lucian so it's showing me possessed people," I announced to the group.

"This is great. The Remnant won't realise that we know they are possessed so we have the upper hand now," suggested Jess.

"We should make sure it works correctly at a longer range before celebrating. Perhaps visiting the local village I can finally rid the place from this plague of monstrosities," suggested Ophanim.

Dalton did not look best pleased by this suggestion.

"With all due respect, Mr Ophanim, I believe we have completed our participation in this venture, and given the circumstances back in your time we must be dealing with the complete closure of the time portals," he argued.

"My time, Meier? My time is now, here with all of you, possibly even more than you. I have outlived your ancestors! There are Remnant down there right now capable of opening the portal for themselves. The best thing to do would be to stop them from hindering us before continuing on your path to which I honestly must say seems futile. I have spent more years than all your lives put together trying close the portals myself," Ophanim protested angrily.

Bill seemed to find the argument humorous and smirked at both of them.

"Look, the pair of you, will you both just shut up!" Jess insisted, becoming frustrated. We all want the same thing. It won't take two minutes to see if the device works properly, right?" queried Jess looking sternly at Ophanim

"Correct," he replied.

"Well then, let's just get it over with. We don't even know what our next step is anyway so let's do it and try and think of some way of stopping the portals as we go." I could not fault her logic, plus I wanted to try out my device as soon as possible.

"I think she's right. Come on, Dalton, it won't take that long and if there's no more Remnant to worry about then we can work in peace," I said.

Dalton realised he was outvoted and succumb to the democracy of the group. "Well, I'm all for fairness. As long as you all understand what dangers you will be putting yourselves in even with the device and weapons. If anything happens, it's on your heads," he warned.

"Then it is settled. We should leave immediately," Ophanim said heading immediately for the stairwell.

"He really likes to get shit done doesn't he? Think we'd best follow on, lad," suggested Bill patting me on the back.

We followed behind him back up the stone spiral stairwell and I started to realise I had willingly volunteered to put myself in danger to hunt down a couple of Remnant. I should definitely think more before I speak. The further I ventured outside of my normal life the more I realised I could not go back. What would be the point now? My previous life had achieved nothing.

After scaling the stairwell, the group finally ended up back in the piano room.

"May I ask how you managed to discover the secret passage?" enquired Ophanim as the piano slid back over the entrance.

"Well, after you kidnapped Jess we heard a noise from this room, which is when I noticed the dust-covered keys or, more specifically, the keys containing little dust. I then deciphered the melody as Allegro Deciso," explained Dalton with his usual accomplished grin.

"Ahhh, very nicely done, but I grew weary of that melody. You know, after a few hundred times it just becomes… dull. So I just use the open button," replied Ophanim pointing to a small black button on the underside of the piano.

Dalton's face dropped slightly.

"Ha ha, well on the bright side it worked ol' chap," laughed Bill in a patronising tone while patting Dalton's back.

Eventually we made our way out into the night air. I'm not one to be claustrophobic but being outdoors was preferable to the castle's narrow and twisting hallways.

Walking down the foggy pathway toward the small village I looked up at the moon. Unfamiliar colours still danced across the sky masking its usual grey tone. I wouldn't have described my feelings as joyous right now but I guess I was content everyone was alive and I wasn't being chased by demonic creatures. I found myself inspired by the moon and started thinking about that classic song that requires singing to whenever played.

"We get it almost every night," I sang under my breath as the group walked alongside me. Jess gave a brief glance and a smile that conveyed, 'you idiot, Griff'.

"And when that moon is big and bright…" I sang a little louder.

"… it's a supernatural delight!" Bill added to my surprise, catching up to me.

"Everybody's dancing in the moonlight!" we sang in a terrible duet.

"Would you both be silent? We don't know who could be listening," instructed Dalton. What a killjoy, nobody was even around.

"Hey, at least we look a little more normal like this than a suspicious group walking silently down to a village in the middle of the night. It's not like they're expecting us," complained Bill. I thought his point was fairly valid.

"At the very least sing something tasteful. Perhaps Louis Armstrong or Nina Simone," Dalton retorted.

Gate hopping the wooden picket entrance to the castle we made our way through the open marketplace and then down the main road.

Watching carefully at the arrow's position on my wrist it began to rotate as we wandered toward a large building about three houses wide and four floors up with a wooden balcony above. I peered up to a signpost.

Bran New Hotel

It was a good play on words, I'll give them that.

"This is our stop," I whispered to the group who had gathered behind me.

"You kidding me? Another hotel? Can none of them rent?" complained Bill.

"So one of those Remnant or possessed people are inside there?" asked Jess.

"Looks like it. The light's still on. Do we just go in?" I questioned.

"To remain inconspicuous I would advise Mr Holster and Miss Hart enter alone, playing the role of a couple checking in. I believe we may give the game away if an assorted group such as ourselves entered together," suggested Dalton.

"His logic makes sense. You both go in and scout the place while we remain outside ready to pounce on any unsuspecting Remnant foes," Ophanim added.

Jess looked at me and shrugged her shoulders in a sort of hesitant agreement. I wasn't exactly the best actor. Oh well, what choice did I have? If anything went wrong I had backup so, for once, I wasn't too worried.

"Alright then but you had better be ready if we need you."

"Don't worry, Griff. I'll save you if I have to," smiled Bill with an idiotic cheesy grin and a thumbs up. I rolled my eyes in pessimism.

The large cracked wooden front door was open. Jess and I entered together, trying to be as calm as possible. The small chime of a bell tingled as the door knocked opened but nobody came to greet us.

Inside was a rustic old reception desk with an outdated computer and large leather ledger perched on top. Buzzing came from the out of place fluorescent lighting above as we approached the desk. I placed my left arm on top of the counter and kept my right arm and the device concealed underneath the wooden desk whilst leaning forward.

Ding, Ding!

Jess tapped the small golden bell, ringing it twice and leaning casually up against the counter next to me.

"This place is amazing, Griff. I can't believe you brought me here," Jess teased. I just frowned and shook my head.

Eventually the sound of footsteps could be heard coming from a small corridor behind the desk. A shadow lurked around the corner before a tall figure appeared. The arrow on the device followed his motion perfectly toward the desk, blinking faster as he came closer.

Gazing up from the device the man was the same height as myself but built like some kind of superhuman. His jaw was squared which matched his square black haircut. It was like looking at a polarised version of Bill.

"Va pot ajuta?" he said in a burly voice.

Standing speechless I was glad Jess managed to speak up.

"Sorry do you speak English?" She asked in a calm gentle voice.

He squinted slightly. "Check in?" he asked after a short hesitation.

"Yes, please, that would be great. We're on our honeymoon," she added, trying to make a plausible backstory.

"Yeah, I wanted to go to Hawaii but the missus was just dying to come here for some reason," I joked awkwardly.

Clearly the large man did not understand us and just stared with his huge white eyes. I definitely did not feel comfortable.

"Wait here," he commanded as he walked back down the corridor.

The arrow followed him back out of the room.

"What are you doing, Griff? Act natural for Christ's sake," Jess instructed nudging me in the side.

"I'm trying, but he's one of them." I glared at her.

"What? He's possessed?"

"Well, according to this thing on my wrist he is" I told her.

"Damn, he's huge. We'd better get the others."

"Wait, we have to make sure first. We don't just want to kill randomly."

Before we had the chance to make a move he arrived back from the side corridor at the desk. There was a silent exchange of stares as he stopped still in front of us. Another shadow glided across the corridor wall.

"How long you stay?" questioned the receptionist dropping papers in front of us.

Jess picked one up. It looked like some kind of check-in sheet.

"I don't understand this, it's in Romanian," Jess informed the giant. He looked frustrated. Jess went to hand him the paper back but then purposely cut him with it along the hand.

"Oops sorry," she said, grinning awkwardly.

The man shrugged it off but did not look best pleased as he lurched away. A couple of seconds later he returned with another form in his hands and as he went to hand it to Jess I noticed the cut was not even bleeding.

"Actually I think we may have the wrong place. Sorry to have taken up your time," explained Jess putting on a nervy smile whilst backing off from the desk.

A man slightly smaller in stature but equal in muscle mass arrived behind the reception desk. My wrist device arrow was flashing side to side unable to pick out a target. They must both be possessed.

"Yeah, I think we were meant to be in the other Bran hotel, so we will just be going now." I pointed over my shoulder toward the door.

"There is no other hotel." The second man, who had a much better use of English, glared.

"No pack," pointed out the first man to the second pointing to the floor. He obviously meant backpack.

Jess's eyes quickly skipped from me to them repeatedly, searching for a signal to do something but I panicked, my mouth opened but no words came out.

My eyes flickered up and down from the two men to the wrist device while the smaller man opened up a wooden board on the reception desk allowing him access to us.

Leaning forward the larger man attempted to peer over the desk to see what I kept looking at. His eyes opened wide in a cold lifeless stare, his mouth gaped and let out the shrill, horrifying, Remnant screech.

"Run!" I yelled.

Fire.

Crack. Whistle

Wooden splinters erupted from a circular hole in the desk as the shot from the wrist device tore through it and up through the man's lower abdomen. His expression turned to that of someone about to vomit as the other man staggered with surprise. The beam continued through the man before continuing through the wall behind him, leaving a perfectly circular opening.

Bang, bang!

Jess fired two shots from her pistol directly into the second man's face tearing off part of his cheek and leaving a hole in the side of his forehead. Sickeningly this did not stop him.

Backing off from the desk I was met by the smaller man sprinting full force, tackling me into the door which instantly gave way, flying open and smashing violently against the wall. Landing flat on my back I barely felt any pain as the electrical charge from the device pumped through my veins. Blood treacled down from the man's shocking injuries and dripped onto my face as he bared down on me. Kicking out I managed to throw him off.

Rising up at my feet he towered in front of the doorway casting a shadow across me, looking down in disgust and anger. He tried to take a step toward me when a hail of bullets pierced through his chest.

Dropping to his knees he clutched the mass of wounds now pouring with blood. Bill appeared from behind him grasping his weapon which smoked from the barrel in the cold air. Looking up at Bill the man was met with a final merciless bullet to the forehead causing him to collapse to one side.

"Mother fucker," Bill commented under his breath. The possessed man emitted a red glow which flurried off into the fresh night air.

Back up on my feet I pointed toward the doorway.

"Cheers, Bill. There's another one in there with Jess!" I hastily explained.

Lights flickered as it was obvious there was a commotion inside the building. Gunshots cracked through the silent night echoing into nothingness.

The larger figure stumbled out of the doorway, light shining through a gaping space where part of his body had once been. Red fluid drained down his legs staining his worn jeans. Another two gunshots were fired and the man collapsed upon the lifeless body of his friend.

Dalton and Jess appeared in the doorway

"Quite the commotion you have caused," announced Dalton as the red smoke lifted from the man's remains.

"You should have allowed me to deal with them quietly! Now others will know of our presence, and bear down on us!" shouted an annoyed Ophanim.

"Oooh, so sorry. I guess we should have just used our fists to kill the huge super humans trying to murder us," retaliated Jess.

DING. DING. DING.

Chapter 9

When the Bell Tolls

After killing two possessed people and making an extremely loud racket, it was no surprise to me that there would be terrible consequences. I was under the impression that there would only be a couple of people who were possessed and that it would only be a matter of taking out a few stray Remnant. Turns out I was wrong.

Bell rings cracked through the silent night echoing into the distance. Lights turned on in nearby buildings alerted to our presence. Faces of all varieties peeked through curtains to see what the commotion was. The cat was well and truly out of the bag.

"I thought there was only a few of them?"

"I may have under-estimated the numbers. It has been a while since I scouted the area," replied Ophanim.

"Well, I certainly feel a little more pessimistic about our current state of affairs," said Dalton.

"Think maybe we should get back to the castle?" questioned Jess.

Shadows began appearing through the viscous fog between buildings. Torch lights beamed down the pathways accompanied by the sound of footsteps.

"That could be a good idea," agreed Bill.

"Whatever happens try to return to the castle and rendezvous in the main entrance," instructed Dalton.

What I can only describe as a small hoard of people began running at us from the end of the pathway. It was like seeing a rival faction after a football match. I swear I could feel a twinge of phantom pain where my cheek had scarred.

"Shit, leg it!" yelled Bill setting off at full pace in the opposite direction and scooting down a side alley.

He definitely had the right idea as the swathes of people closed in on our position – it looked like half the town was after us. Chimes from the bell continued to echo through the dark night sky.

Running after Bill I zigzagged between buildings trying to keep him in my sight. I had taken my pistol in my hands to make use of the flashlight attachment while circumnavigating the dimly lit areas.

Checking behind me only Jess was following. Dalton and Ophanim must have chosen a different route. It would make sense that Ophanim would know the fastest and safest way back but there was no time to debate that now or change direction.

My wrist device indicator was going wild, pointing this way and that, it didn't know where it wanted to be, although the two blue charging lights had turned off. Before I could make it any further I spotted Bill get tackled to the ground ahead of me. Quickly crouching on one knee I took aim with the pistol.

Crack. Whistle.

To my complete surprise the wrist device decided to go off at the same time as the gun, firing a beam of the gravitational energy through the assailant shoulder to shoulder. His head freed from his body and fell onto Bill's chest while the rest of his body flopped to one side pooling blood on the floor. Red mist seeped through the corpse and up into the air.

"Fucking hell!" shouted an enraged Bill, throwing the severed head from his chest.

Jess had caught up to the commotion as Bill stood himself up.

"Jesus, Griff!" exclaimed Jess staring at the gory mess on the floor.

"I didn't know it would fire," I insisted.

"You two, hurry up. They're still after us!" yelled Bill running off once more.

Electrical charges burst through my body once more like an intense sugar rush.

"We can take them!" I shouted over to Bill who was already some way ahead of us. I knew it was a bad choice but the rush from the device made me feel up for a fight. I wanted to kill them and my body was urging me to run back but my brain was contradicting.

"Have you gone loopy, Griff? Stop being an idiot and come on!" yelled Jess who had followed Bill into the distance.

"Ahhh!" I exhaled through gritted teeth shaking my head clear.

I sprinted after my companions. They turned a corner ahead and following at full velocity I turned the same corner and saw Bill and Jess heading back up toward the castle, they had almost made it to the marketplace. Just ahead of me turning in from the opposite corner were more of the possessed villagers facing my two friends.

"Balls!"

Before they had the chance to see me I was tugged from behind and ended up being dragged into the building next to me.

Under the influence of the device I managed to throw myself free from the grasp inside the doorway. Scrambling away I turned and stood up to view my assailant. Pointing my gun directly at him I was confronted by an older couple looking slightly too terrified to be possessed – or so I assumed.

"Nu trage! Nu trage!" The grey haired man yelled at me holding his hands in the air as the woman closed the door peeping out of the curtains.

"I don't understand you. Calm down will you?" The elderly man seemed almost hysterical.

Lowering my gun seemed to placate him. My wrist device indicator was going crazy, pointing all over the place as shadows floated past outside. The arrow never pointed directly at either of the couple but I still couldn't trust them, after all, the whole town was after me, what made these two special? They were the first proper Romanians I had seen who were possibly not possessed, dressed like normal people in bland jumpers and jeans.

"Steregoi," whispered the man pointing out the window.

I looked at him confused. Never in my life had I thought Romanian would be a language that would come in handy.

"The Remnant?" I asked pointing out the window.

"Steregoi," he repeated nodding his head.

The woman began ushering me into the hallway, gently shoving me in the back.

"Woah woah woah! I need to get back to my friends! The big castle!" I tried explaining while moulding the air into the shape of the castle with my hands.

"Castle?" she questioned with a worried stare.

"Yes! Bran Castle. I need to get up there."

At this point the man had joined us and wandered over to a door under the stairs. Opening it revealed a tiny wardrobe filled with jackets and shoes.

"I'm not hiding. I've told you I need to go." I tried explaining again becoming frustrated at the lack of communication. The man returned my frustrated look before shoving the assortment of footwear to one side and pulling up the old muddied rug revealing a trap door with a large black cross painted centrally. Pulling on a circular cast handle the door lifted open revealing a flimsy wooden ladder leading down into a blackened hole. I was not expecting any locals to be left unpossessed and it did not matter to me right now how this couple avoided being captured. What was important was that they were helping me escape and I had no other choice in the matter.

Descending down the damp ladder I reached the gravel floor. Waving my pistol around I tried to gain a good look at my surroundings. In front of me was a system of humid catacombs twisting and turning in every direction.

"Urma!" came a voice from above. I peered upwards pointing my light toward the man who was hanging down through the trapdoor. He was pointing to the wall where a cast iron image of a tower on a hill was visible. There were other metallic signs next to it but I did not pay them any attention.

"Castle!" he shouted pointing again.

"Alright, I got you, mate. Cheers!" I shouted back up.

The cast signs must lead to different areas. Who knew how long these catacombs had been in use? I heard heavy banging from the front door above.

"Hey! What about you?" I shouted up.

With a worried look the man disappeared out of the hole and the light vanished as the trap door was shut.

"I'd better get a move on," I whispered to myself. Air condensed in a cloud in the torch light as I breathed.

I looked about to find the passageway with the correct sign posted on it. There it was to my right leading in the direction of the castle. I made my way casually down the passage, careful not to trip or smash my head on one of the wooden beams that supported the walls and ceilings.

Every few minutes the tunnels split off into different sections but there was always a sign hanging from the wall to guide me like a trail of bread crumbs. Sometimes the tunnels were thin and I could barely squeeze through, but then they also expanded outwards into large house-sized expanses. From upwards to downwards, left and right I was getting myself lost further into the labyrinth.

Pressing the small button on the square device on my collar, all I received was a large bout of static. Radios probably don't work very well underground I should have realised.

Up ahead I spotted a ray of moonlight entering the tunnel. A smile grew on my face as I jogged a little faster toward the glow. The sound of crashing water came into earshot as I closed in. My joy was short lived as I entered a large cavern the size of a church hall. One of the supports had given away to the right and water was gushing in from an opening at an alarming rate forming a small turbulent river spanning fifteen feet across the room.

It looked too treacherous to swim over as I would be instantly sucked away into wherever the water led. Trekking back would be pretty useless, I would end up exiting somewhere unknown, lost and vulnerable to attack.

"Why is nothing ever simple?!" I yelled into the cave.

Examining the puzzle in my wake I scratched my head thinking of how to cross the river. A large section of wooden beam lay destroyed next to the waterfall. It was already balanced over the edge of the water, maybe I could use it to cross. I placed my gun in my holster as the glow from the waterfall entrance was enough to see by.

I found the beam too heavy to even contemplate throwing it to the other side and realised it wasn't long enough to reach anyway. When I pushed it over into the water the currents sucked it down the opposite side of the room where it proceeded to get battered into oblivion before its remains were sucked down into the hole.

"OK, so swimming is definitely out of the question," I muttered. Talking to myself was becoming a habit – maybe this whole experience really was turning me crazy.

There had to be some way, I couldn't just be stuck here. Stepping toward the far wall where the flowing water met the wall I checked for any means to climb over but the surface was flat and slippery. Putting my right hand up against the surface it was clear there was nothing to hold onto. Then again looking at my wrist maybe I could create my own surface to climb along, one down the bottom for my feet and one above for my hands.

Placing the device against the wall at head height my arm was contorted in a strange uncomfortable way. The cross hairs were poised on the opposite wall. Fire.

Crack, Whistle.

A smooth line cut into the wall leaving a semi cylindrical gap to grasp. One of the support beams cracked on the opposite side of the river creating a worrying groaning noise and causing dirt to flutter from the ceiling. I stood staring without a breath until the groaning subsided. Exhaling a huge sigh of relief, I looked toward creating the foothold. Gripping hold of the ledge I raised my feet to see if it was sturdy to hold my weight. Shuffling a couple feet across the wall I decided I could do without the foothold. I felt invincible once again under the charge of the device.

Stretching further across the river with every grasp, I was making good progress with my feet propped up against the wall but as I reached two thirds of the way over I heard that dreaded groaning noise once more. Peering over to the beam, a crack had formed in the wall and was slowly opening up, bending and weaving toward the ridge I had made.

"Nope! Don't you dare!" I argued with the growing fissure.

Increasing my speed was a mistake as the charge had worn off and caused me to misread my next hold. Slipping across the wall I was hanging by one hand my feet sprayed by the mist of the crashing water below. Staring up to the crack I utilised a final burst of strength to push myself off the wall with both feet and leapt across the final section of water.

Rolling across the floor the crack met the ledge I had made and the floor began rumbling as a cross section of the wall collapsed down in front of me. The debris came to a halt at my feet. I felt unbelievably lucky. Observing the mess I had created I saw that the hole which the water ran down was now blocked causing the water to instantaneously rise and flow down the tunnel I had just come from, like a giant waterslide.

I thought nothing of it as I was just relieved to have made it across. Picking myself up from the mud-drenched floor I headed further down the tunnel system. Listening to my feet crunch on the drying rocky floor was starting to drive me mad but luckily it did not take too long to reach another ladder leading up to a wooden hatch.

Climbing I could feel the chill of the cold outside. A firm shove was enough to slide the hatch over to one side. The brisk breeze hit me but the air was refreshing after being stuck in the stuffy humid catacombs for so long. Taking in a large breath I was free.

Chapter 10

Unwelcoming

So I was hoping that everyone had made it safely to the castle and that it would just be a case of them all waiting for me to arrive and we could all hide in Ophanims little lair and find a way to stop the Remnant and Angious. That is what I was hoping. What I was making myself believe was completely different – that someone had been caught or that I would get back to the castle and once again not be trusted by my friends and be accused of being possessed.

Spinning on the spot I turned to face Bran Castle. I had exited the tunnels directly behind the castle in the forest. The hatch had been hidden by shrubbery which was moved to the side when I pushed it open. Kicking the wooden hatch over, I closed it again and pushed the shrubbery over to conceal its presence.

Wandering up to the castle I hoped everything would be fine for once, it would be a nice change. I tried the radio again and this time there was no back feed through the speaker.

"Hello, is anyone in the castle? Where is everyone?" I enquired.

ROOOOOAAARRR!

I froze on the spot in terror. It was not the usual sound of the Remnant. Something else was behind me and wanted me to know it. Turning slowly around I caught the eye of an extremely deadly looking brown bear about fifty feet away, brown fur waving in the breeze and a puff of wet air exiting its nostrils. Great, exactly what I needed right now.

"Griff! Get yourself to the castle right no….." I clicked the mute button on the radio without making too much of a sudden movement.

ROOOAARRR!

It climbed up on its rear legs standing much taller than myself. I think right now I was probably more frightened than if any Remnant had attacked me. Not for the fact that this is indeed a deadly creature but because I really didn't want to harm it. It doesn't know I could kill it. I had my gun and my wrist device and it wouldn't even be an inconvenience to me. Inside though, it felt heartless to do so. There are evil beings out there but a bear passing in the woods is not evil. I was in its home, I am the trespasser, I am the criminal.

Tilting its head at me I kept complete eye contact. I had seen a documentary on bears and was pretty sure for brown bears I had to stay completely still. I did not see any smaller bears around which would work in my favour. With no cubs to protect, it would be more likely to leave me alone.

"Go on, fella. Get yourself out of here," I whispered under my breath trying not to move my face.

Paws slammed to the ground so that it was back on all fours. Huffing again the mist of its breath plumed in the air. I stared it down. Seeing directly into its brown eyes I did not see hatred, I did not see menacing evil. There was just life. Life I did not want to extinguish.

"Please…" I whispered again.

Hesitantly the bear gave a last muffled roar and stumbled away to one side. Walking casually into the forest I watched the bear closely as I remained stuck firmly to the spot. Allowing it to vanish I gave a huge sigh of relief.

Scaling up the side of the hill I hauled my way up to the castle entrance where I found the door still open. Gently and quietly I made my way through the doorway and turned to face the room with the giant painting.

Entering the room quietly as not to be ambushed, I was met by a sight which did not build confidence. Ophanim was standing upright, posed perfectly with his sword nestled against Bill's neck as Jess held her firearm directed straight toward Ophanim's chest in a frozen standoff.

"Now what the hell is going on? What's the crack?" I asked bounding into the room.

Jess remained focused on Ophanim but Bill looked at me with worried eyes.

"Griff lad, thank God you're here, can you prove to this nutter that we are not possessed," Bill requested with a drop of sweat running from his forehead.

"Great isn't it, when you come back and your friends attack and suspect you?" I replied sarcastically as I recalled escaping the power plant on the island just to be attacked by Bill.

"Don't be a dick, Griff, get over here!" instructed Jess annoyed.

"Alright, alright," I answered rolling my eyes as I casually walked over to the group.

The arrow remained pointing the opposite direction as I first passed Bill and then Jess.

"It's all clear, Ophanim, you can stop being paranoid now," I suggested.

Ophanim lowered his sword in a swift move and slid it into its sheath.

"I have been around far too long to make such a simple mistake. Which is why I am not prepared to make it," he explained. Jess also lowered her weapon happy that the situation had been resolved so swiftly.

"What happened, Griff? How did you get away?" she asked showing instant concern for my wellbeing.

"I was cut off by another hoard of people and some locals pulled me into a house. They showed me an underground catacomb place which led me here. Pretty lucky, really," I explained in a nutshell.

"That is it! I knew they had a way of disappearing," Ophanim said.

"You didn't see Dalton did ya?" Bill asked rubbing his neck.

"Na, why? Is he not here?" I asked.

"Well I don't see him, do you?" replied Bill with sarcasm.

I looked at him sternly.

"Next time I'm letting him lop your head off."

"Maybe he hid downstairs, we should check there," suggested Jess.

"Good idea, we'll go down and have a butchers'," agreed Bill.

"A butchers?" inquired Ophanim.

"Yeah, like, we will go have a look," I explained.

"Ahhhh I see. I concur but maybe Miss Hart should stay up here in case Mr Dalton does return."

"Sure, I could use a nice sit down anyway." Jess smiled as she parked herself in one of the medieval-looking black chairs.

"Right, let's go. We have a German illuminati guy to find, can't be that hard!" Bill exclaimed as he began wandering up the stairs.

The three of us walked from room to room pretty casually, not in a completely relaxed way but without the fear of immediate danger.

Some of the rooms remained lit from the previous visit, some lights turned on by Ophanim knowing the complete layout of the building off by heart. It only took a minute to wander up the secret bookcase passage into the piano room.

"Would you like to do the honours?" Bill asked gesturing toward the piano.

Pressing the button on the underside of the piano opened up the secret passage. For some reason the torches on the walls were now lit. It was concerning although perhaps it was Dalton lighting the way down. Instinctively I pulled back my sleeve checking the wrist device. The arrow was going crazy as we began our descent into the capsule room. We had almost reached the bottom when the dreaded Remnant screech echoed through the darkened stairwell sending shivers down my spine. I did not have to inform the other two of the imminent threat, it was more than obvious now.

Reaching the bottom the last flame torch on the stairwell was the only form of light at the entrance as almost the entire room was drowned in sheer blackness.

"I don't like this at all," Bill stated.

Bill and I used our torches to shine beams of light through the chilled fogged up room. Ophanim grabbed the last torch from the wall. The only other flicker of light was the ray of moonlight coming from the ceiling reflecting down to form the portal on the opposite side of the room. Monitoring the gateway closely a blackened tar-covered Remnant entered the cage. Before I knew it the beast slowly phased to one side into the darkness and out of sight.

"Ohhh shit! What's happened?" I asked, extremely worried.

The fact that the portal was open must mean that the cage was open as well. There could be any number of Remnant climbing about the place, stalking us in the darkness. Their thermal vision in such a cold climate would prove to be an extreme advantage with Ophanim's torch giving off mass amounts of heat like a giant target. Not only was it dark but the misty fog directed the beams of light into more narrow channels.

"It is imperative we act now. We must close that portal down," Ophanim replied.

"This is what happens when you mess around with shit instead of just getting rid of the problem in the first place!" Bill angrily accused.

"Shhhhh. Fuckin' hell, Bill, keep it down," I commanded.

"It does not matter, they already know we are here. They will be waiting for the best time to strike, be vigilant," recommended Ophanim as he paced slowly toward the console.

Through the light beams dark shadows played against the walls. A single droplet of thickened black liquid collapsed onto the floor between Bill and Ophanim. Shining my Light upwards I caught the back end of scaly legs frantically scattering across the ceiling before evading my sight.

"They're circling around us." I began breathing heavily, panic setting in.

Claw marks were strewn across the pillars; marks that could so easily be etched into one of our bodies as soon as they decided to attack. To be honest this is probably the most frightened I have ever been in my life. Somewhere in the darkness was a monster about to try to kill me and I had no clue where and when it would attack. I felt sick.

Both my heartbeat and breathing seemed to be abnormal, missing beats and loosing volume. Ophanim had his sword in one hand the torch in another, Bill had his rifle and I had my wrist device and pistol. Walking closer as a tight group we aimed toward the console surrounded by demonic enemies. Dear God, how did I get myself into this kind of situation? What was I thinking?

Suddenly the room erupted in a hail of bullets as Bill launched a ferocious barrage into the fog. I was almost deafened by the sound. This was followed by a horrifyingly close roar from the Remnant. I turned pointing my light at the pillar which was littered with compact bullet holes. Blue blood was present but a body was not.

Clattering of glass sounded from the opposite side. I spun once again and the menacing face of Lucian peered at me. On complete instinct I shot without even giving myself two seconds to aim.

Crack, Whistle.

Wood and glass fractured into pieces as I completely demolished the laboratory equipment laid out on a table. Lucian disappeared into darkness. I had no idea if I had injured him or not, or maybe he wasn't even there and I was seeing visions in the dark, it wouldn't surprise me the punishing rate blood was being pumped through my body. Now with the added charge boost from the device it felt like time was slowing down. My fingertips were tingling and I felt like I must be overdosing.

Ophanim reached the console and in a flash the four crystal pillars in the corners of the room flared up into bright glowing light illuminating every space. It was not as reassuring as I had hoped, as scores of Remnant bodies twitched and traversed the frosty walls and ceiling.

Multiple roars erupted from all directions as the monsters bared tooth and claw.

"Good that I have practiced," announced Ophanim with a concentrated face. He had dropped his flame and steadied both hands on his sword.

With little time to react the beasts launched an attack from all sides. Time seemed slow from the adrenaline and charge running through my body. Three of the blackened Remnant headed toward Ophanim in unison. Phasing and leaping through the air they were upon him in seconds. Without hesitation Ophanim timed his swing, perfectly slicing one of the Remnant's claws off with one swipe. Continuing on from this he swivelled his blade to lung backwards directly into the heart of the Remnant approaching from behind. Kicking the beast from the blade its chest erupted in a fountain of blue blood. The third creature lunged to take a bite from Ophanim, but swaying on the spot he dodged and with unbelievable precision and timing pulled the sword from the floor cutting from one end of the being to the other. Both halves of the Remnant fell either side of Ophanim dousing him in a shower of blood. The first Remnant that had attacked stood armless, watching with a snarl. Letting out a horrific cry as blood drew from the two stumps at the ends of its arms was all it could do before Ophanim rounded off his overly impressive efforts with a firm swipe across the demon's neck. Dropping to the floor in a heap next to the remains of the other two Remnants I stood aghast, not able to comprehend such abilities.

Almost deafened by a hail of gunfire I flinched to one side. Bill had just fired a storm of lead into a Remnant attempting to lunge at me while I was mesmerised.

"Stop fucking about, Griff! Shoot these bastards!" screamed Bill into my ear angered at my hesitation.

Another beast pounced behind Bill, its teeth baring brilliant white. My reactions were increased from the charge as I began paying more attention to my surroundings. Pulling my weapon to chest height I shot three times into the Remnant's heart area. It twitched and faltered, dropping to a heap on the floor, phasing while blood oozed from smouldering holes. I felt satisfaction.

"We must close the portal before we become overwhelmed!" shouted Ophanim over the sound of claws scraping stone. He proceeded to throw the flaming torch at an aggressive Remnant which was unscathed by the heat but lost its bearings just long enough for Ophanim to slice through its heart.

Closing the portal was easier said than done. We had taken out a few of them but they were swarming in through the portal in great numbers, leaving black resin across the floor and walls which dripped from the gouges created by their monstrous claws.

Ophanim took front point as Bill and I covered the sides from any flanking enemies. They kept on swarming from all sides in an unending onslaught. Gunfire hailed across the room tearing through Remnant bodies lodging lead into the walls, piping hot shell casings cascaded to the floor sounding like faint bell chimes. Ophanim's blade slid through Remnant bodies with ease, he was far too fast for them and with us covering they had no chance of sneaking up on him.

"Get a fucking move on, lads, it's not like they're stopping for a break!" commanded Bill with authority.

We had only a few feet left in front of us to the portal levers on the wall when we descended into chaos. One of the shadows had managed to elude us, dropping down from above, directly in the centre of our compact triangle. With one large swing of its claw, Bill was knocked clear of the group right in front of the portal, a red patch instantly formed on his waist. Ophanim engaged with the enemy while I ran toward Bill.

The black goop on the wall slowly deformed, pushing outward, dripping slowly to the floor. Another Remnant had escaped Helvius and was directly in front of Bill who was dazed and in pain. It turned and faced me, the tar melting from its face like some extra hideous deformation. I did not understand what was happening at first as it raised its arms but as the mastic cleared I saw the clear outline of an Angious rifle.

"What the f–"

It shot a blast at me. That was it, I was done for. My luck had finally run out. I pushed my arm up in front of myself as if it would shield me. The blue lights on my device had cleared away. Green lights whizzed toward me. About a foot away they dissipated into a stream of aurora style lights in a dome around me, only for a split second… What had happened? Why was I not the equivalent of a slice of Swiss cheese?

I did not dwell on the thought but raised my arm further upwards. Fire. Tar and blood and bone cracked and twisted as the beast's arm tore from the shoulder. Dropping the weapon with the severed limb it staggered back into the portal. Thank God.

"Nice shot lad you saved my life." Bill was kneeling on one leg and in pain next to the portal. He picked up the Angious weapon with a more pleasant look on his face while placing the old rifle to the floor.

I had let my guard down too soon. Tar burst from the portal as a claw dug its way out, crunching down and impaling Bill's leg. He let out air in anguish. He made no scream just the loss of breath. My eyes widened. Ohh, God, no.

That was it, no time to react. Bill was instantly dragged through the portal shooting his Angious rifle and without any extra word, he had vanished. For a brief moment scenes of Jasper's demise flashed through my mind.

Chapter 11

Different Agenda

"NOOOO!" I yelled almost losing my voice.

I sprinted toward the portal not thinking correctly. I had to get Bill, I HAD TO. I pushed my body toward the blackened stain on the wall. My body crushed into itself as I thumped against solid stone. Breath left my body unexpectedly as I fell backwards onto the floor – I had completely winded myself. I coughed erratically trying to regain oxygen.

Wheezing I managed to peer up to my side where Ophanim had his hand on the lever, he had shut the portal with Bill on the other side.

"What have you done…?" I coughed, wide eyed. Sickened inside, it felt like my heart had grown double in size, weighted my chest and was blocking my windpipe. I felt panic.

"What had to be done, Griffin. He was dead the instant he left this plane of existence." He tried to explain himself in a calm and collected manner. I, on the other hand, was not in such a cooperative mood.

"You killed him…. THAT'S WHAT YOU'VE DONE!" My eyes swelled up as I pointed at the wall.

"No, he could not possibly survive the environment without a suit," Ophanim tried to explain.

"How the fuck do you know?! Have you been on the other side? He could heal faster on that side like they do on this side!" I yelled at him using the Remnant as a reference. I saw red. The mist descended over my eyes completely. I picked myself up in a rage.

"You absolute dickhead!" I yelled aiming a fist at his face. He dodged with ease and I flew by falling to the floor with the momentum of my poorly attempted punch. I hit the ground with force. I pushed myself up once again resting my back against the wall looking up at him.

"You fucking killed him," I panted. I could feel my eyes trying to water up but managed to supress any visual evidence of how upset I was; I just wanted him to see my anger.

"Jesus, what happened? Are you alright?" Jess enquired as she approached us.

"Not even a little bit," I answered looking down at the floor.

"Where's Bill?" she asked worried.

"Yeah. Where is Bill?" I glared up at Ophanim disgusted.

He seemed hesitant at first to answer, looking back and forth to where the portal once was.

"We were ambushed by the Remnant beasts, the portal had been activated and we had to close it. Your friend was... He was dragged through the portal... I had to shut it to prevent more Remnant arriving. I had to do it there was no other choice," he explained.

"There is always a choice, you prick!" I screamed at him.

Rising from the floor in fury Jess had to grab me before I could attempt another swing at Ophanim.

"What ya doing, Jess? Let me go!" I yelled. My brain had lost all control of my body, until I looked into Jess's eyes and saw tears forming. One ran down her cheek and I calmed.

"He knew what dangers there were, Griff. You can't blame Ophanim for this, we need each other... I knew Bill way before you, he knew what could happen, the price he may have to pay."

I inhaled a deep breath trying my best to prevent the quiver on my lip as I suppressed rage and grief.

"He's gone, Jess..." I let go of Jess and stared at the cold floor.

Even though I had not known the man for very long I still thought of him as a very close friend. After being through all this mess together he was someone I could trust and rely on. Maybe what struck me most was not the fact that he was gone but that I had let him down. I felt I could rely on him and he probably thought the same of me, but I had let him down.

"My deepest sympathies.... I'm so sorry it had to be," Ophanim said quietly.

"Shut your Goddamn mouth!" I snapped.

"You know Bill never trusted you to begin with and now I can understand why." I expressed my thoughts to the group.

Letting out a broken sigh I took in the scene of bullet ridden walls and smashed wooden tables. Black goop had hardened on the various surfaces glimmering in the light of the console.

"We should check the rooms to make sure there are no Remnant left. I could have sworn I saw Lucian during the fight," I said, walking over and picking up Bills discarded rifle and slinging it across my chest. Ophanim looked at me sternly.

"That's impossible, he was locked away," he explained walking hurriedly toward the room that should have contained him.

We followed behind, the door was swinging loosely on its hinges scarred from the claws of a Remnant. Ophanim recklessly kicked the door in and entered the room alone.

"LUCIAN!" he yelled, rampaging around the room. "No, this is impossible."

Puzzled I observed as Ophanim inspected the cage which should have contained Lucian. It was completely open with no damage. Someone or something must have opened the cage from the outside.

Leaving the room we walked to the opposite side.

"This makes no sense," Ophanim muttered.

"Let's check the other rooms," Jess suggested, her voice light. She went toward the metallic door on the far left of the room which should have housed the captured Remnant. The metallic door was also shredded around the handle which was completely missing. Putting her whole body behind her arms she pushed the door open with a screech.

Inside was another one of the cryocell cages constructed by Ophanim to maintain the Remnant. The stone floor was a wreck as large slabs were littered around a hole on the outside of the cage. It was obvious that the Remnant had burrowed its way below its prison and escaped to release Lucian. They were more intelligent than suspected.

Ophanim examined the hole bending down on one knee. "How?" he asked himself.

"How? Can you not see this is your fault? You underestimated them. You thought you were smarter than them. You judged them on research as if they are all the same. They might look like beasts but they had you well tricked. Through human history there's always been people able to break out of prisons. You didn't think that each individual Remnant could think differently and one might just suss how to get out. Ignorance is idiocy mate," I walked back out of the room feeling better from my rant.

That was probably one of the smartest things I had ever said although, thinking about it, I did not feel very proud as it would help nobody in our current situation. Strange I could think so clearly while I was still in a state of anger and grief. Bill hadn't fully trusted Ophanim and now I felt the same.

Remembering Lucian being threatened by the chamber I wanted to see for myself what Ophanim really was doing down in this dungeon of his. Marching over to the opposite side of the room I went for the furthest door.

"No, Griffin! Remove yourself!" shouted Ophanim as he spotted me.

Sprinting over I didn't have time to mess around. Not even the Remnant had touched this room so there must be something very sinister behind it for them to be afraid. Pointing my device at the door handle I fired.

Crack, Whistle.

Splintered wood was sucked into the gravitational field and my body filled up with energy. I was high on electricity. Tucking my shoulder in I smashed with all my efforts against the door bashing it wide open. Tumbling through I regained my footing and was able to take in the room's layout.

Wide-eyed I took in the dreadful scene. Centring the room was some form of old metallic dentist's chair covered menacingly in dried brown blood. Further brown stains surrounded the chair running toward a drain in the floor. Around the outside of the room were wooden shelves housing giant jars of discoloured liquid. Inside the jars was a complete set of a human brain, spine and heart all still connected. Sickeningly the hearts were all still moving around, twitching, shuffling inside their glass prisons. To the left of the shelves was a workbench with a metal stand holding one of the sets of organs. A metallic claw held a strongly beating heart steady. Probes were hooked up to the brain and heart and the table was covered in surgical utensils and electronic scopes. Next to the bench, on the floor, a wooden box containing dead and discarded organs. Opposite this abomination on the other side of the room was a rack stacked with all kinds of barbaric looking objects, some kind of torture apparatus I would guess. I wouldn't want those things anywhere near me.

Recoiling in shock the damp stench stuck in my throat. I wretched, but was not sick. My own heart beat like crazy. I knew it was from the wrist device charging up but it was like it wanted to crack out my chest and run as far away from this room as possible.

"What the fuck?" I gasped.

Turning around Ophanim was almost next to me, Jess was behind. Instantly seeing that there was something wrong from the expression on my face she raised her weapon at Ophanim's back. Instinctively I raised my own weapon to stop Ophanim in his tracks.

"Get the fuck away from me!" I shouted shaking slightly.

His face was serious. He backed off slightly as I walked out of the room, my face full of disgust.

"Alright, Ophanim. Just what the FUCK is going on in there?!" I demanded.

"What's in there, Griff?" Jess asked.

Ophanim stood for a second, silent.

"I asked you a Goddamn question," I demanded, ignoring Jess's query.

"I… I needed to know how to distinguish between the possessed and human beings. Experimentation was necessary," he tried to explain.

Jess circled around him to view the room as I kept my weapons trained on my target.

"Those things in there are still alive," I said to him.

"Those things are Remnant monsters that kill Angious and humans alike," Ophanim argued.

From the corner of my eye I caught Jess's weapon appear next to mine.

"But to experiment you would have to compare the possessed to human samples right?" asked Jess focusing her weapon at his chest.

"That is correct…" he muttered.

"So you are telling me that some of those things in there were normal human beings! You sick piece of shit!"

BANG!

Ophanim collapsed on one knee as a bullet shattered into his opposing knee. It may not have given him much pain as he has possessed powers but it would have damaged his knee enough to prevent him using it properly.

Jess then fired into him without warning or hesitation again but into his hip.

"Ahhhh! What are you doing!" Ophanim cried out. "Those things are monsters!"

"I think you're confused, mate. Monsters don't get imprisoned and brutally murdered, the monsters do the murdering" I explained.

Jess walked over looking like she was about to execute him on the spot. I wanted to stop her but my subconscious must have wanted him dead as well as I was rooted to the spot. Her gun pressed solidly against his temple for a couple of seconds, her eyes menacingly large. Surprisingly she did not fire her weapon again.

"Stand up, right now!" she ordered.

Ophanim obeyed without another word limping on his good leg.

"Get in the cage," she commanded, waving her pistol toward the back of the room where the portal entrance was located. Again he did as he was instructed. Jess switched the lever over, closing the cage and turning the freeze ability on, trapping him.

"You can stay in there till you rot for all I care," she informed him before walking back over to me.

"You cannot just leave me in here, you need me. I know this place, those monsters," he pleaded.

"Can't you see? You are the monster," I said.

"Unless the next words out of your mouth are the possible locations where the Remnant could have taken Dalton then, believe me, I can definitely leave you here to dehydrate to death, I imagine it would take considerably longer with the way you heal." I knew Jess was a tough girl but I never thought she could be like this.

Ophanim seemed to be genuinely fearful of Jess's threat and I couldn't blame him. Who knew how long and painful it would be to die slowly in this freezing prison. I imagine you would lose your mind first – whatever little he had left.

"Possibly the church. Yes, they could have taken him there, I've seen them sneaking about the place in numbers before," Ophanim said.

"What? The one right next to the castle?" I asked.

"No, the one on the opposite side of the village. They would never dare wander so closely to the castle."

Jess had heard enough, she began walking off toward the spiral staircase on the opposite side of the room. I followed close behind.

"Wait, you can't leave me here!" Ophanim shouted from his cell.

"If we find Dalton at this church, then maybe we let that monster out, if we need him again," Jess said quietly as we exited the room.

Chapter 12

Finding Faith

How could a man bring himself to do such monstrous things – to butcher and mutilate innocent men and women and, God forbid, children in such a way? Who could think to experiment like this could be morally correct? Maybe I keep forgetting that he was not a person, he is a different species masked by a human form. Maybe it was in his nature to be this way or maybe time had gotten the best of his mental health. Either way he was more dangerous than first anticipated.

Furious, depressed and losing hope at an alarming rate, I left the twirling stairwell, but these feelings were more overwhelmed by worry for Jess. She was quiet and looked to be shaking.

Screeching across the floor the piano returned to its inconspicuous position. Jess was already heading for the bookcase passage until I grabbed her arm. She turned with a distant look in her eyes.

"Are you alright?" I asked softly.

She let out a deep breath. "Of course not…"

The words hurt me but I couldn't tell why. She continued down the stairs as if that was the end of the conversation.

"I tried to help him you know," I tried to explain.

"Yes, I know, Griff," she replied, a little more life in her voice but showing no signs of slowing down. "It's just… Bill was the last person I knew from the coastguard and now he is gone. I'm the last one, Griff. And I can't get myself to believe that people can be as evil and sick as Ophanim or as Lucifer was. I know what we are doing is important but my head's a mess. I just don't know what to do."

We had reached the entrance to the castle. Outside was still dark which would help us evade the possessed – the cloak provided by the night was our friend.

"I know this is hard, it's hard for me as well. I really started seeing Bill as a friend, especially after what happened to Jasper and everything on the island. I feel like I've let him down, exactly how I feel like I've let Jasper down, that's the worst part."

Jess watched me intensively as I shared my thoughts. Her expression of sadness and worry moved me to encourage her. We were standing outside the entrance of the castle in the dark cold with a slight wisp of cool air flowing past.

"There are three kinds of people," I continued. "Bad ones, good ones and selfish ones. Now there is no way we are bad, that is for sure, but we don't want to be selfish. We can't be people who rely on others all the time and think the world will just come together; we have to be the good people that stand up and make sure something is done about the bad ones. If we give up, then Jasper, Bill, the people you worked with and all the people on that island and in that chamber down there all died for nothing. If we give up then Dalton is another life lost and the bad guys start outnumbering us even more. We do what we have to do, that's how we make sure they did not die for nothing, and when this is over, then we remember them."

There was a time to grieve; I learned that from Jasper's passing and also from my stupidity trying to run into the portal to follow Bill. I had to keep those feelings inside me until this was over as they would only cause me to make more mistakes when not thinking clearly. There was no way I could do this alone. I needed Jess and I needed Dalton, they were the only two I could trust. Dalton was the only person with enough knowledge on these monsters to get us through this. He would know what to do.

"OK, Griff, let's sneak through these woods, it'll give us more cover than the streets," Jess suggested. She wasn't smiling but at least she now had a sense of direction and purpose.

Journeying through the forests we were careful of the wildlife and to keep as close to the shadows as possible to avoid detection from any lookouts. They were aware of our presence and would undoubtedly be trying to find us or waiting to ambush us. I had informed Jess of my previous bear encounter and of the tunnel system below the village. We could possibly have used the tunnels now, but I had no idea where they would lead us. For all I knew the couple who helped me could have been captured and possessed which would mean they now knew the tunnels existed as well. For me it would be a last resort.

Being careful and moving slowly meant it took slightly longer than anticipated to reach the far end of the forest and the opposite end of the village. The church was visible through the treeline. Compared to Bran Castle this looked a lot more like I was expecting. Bran Castle had been renovated and rebuilt, taking away a lot of its gothic feel whereas this church was very much the horror show I had envisioned.

Stood amongst a bunch of ageing buildings its pointed spire rose up with a long narrow black roof stretching all the way along the main section of the church. A metallic cross perched itself on the tip of the spire overlooking the village. Black stone columns reached up from the floor and supported the sides of the roof whilst eroding gargoyle statues monitored the grounds below. Stained glass windows encompassed the church depicting tales from the bible, obviously some kind of Christian church or something similar, although I had a feeling that whatever was taking place inside was probably not very Christian-like at all. At the back end was a small patch of land covered in tombstones and small crypts – just your average eerie graveyard.

On one side of the spire overlooking the large iron entrance gates was a clock face, possibly the only new part of the building, perhaps replaced recently. Three-forty in the morning. It would be getting light very soon so we had to hurry this along if we had any hope of getting away under the cover of darkness. If Dalton was even inside in the first place.

Going in the front entrance was far too obvious and most likely guarded so we scouted around the premises but there was no other foreseeable way of entering the church. Dumping my behind on a flimsy moss-ridden gravestone I sat hands on knees staring at the medieval structure.

"Well… go out in a hail of gunfire?" Jess questioned, waving her pistol in the air. I could see she didn't really care what we did as long as we did something. It looked like she had pent up rage inside her ready to pop. Unsurprisingly I didn't feel much different, although I still had a decent grasp of reality to know that idea was suicide.

She walked over to crypt opposite me and lent against the side. A statue of the Virgin Mary was looking down from the top of the crypt at the entrance, her hands together praying.

"Any brilliant ideas?" she asked half-heartedly whilst tapping the wall of the grave with her pistol.

I was about to respond when I noticed on the crypt door was a black cross. Half hidden under a combination of moss and ivy it was the exact same cross that was present on both the secret tunnel entrance and behind the castle. Perhaps it was possible. There were symbols in the tunnels for a church – this seemed too good a coincidence.

A small brass ring was attached to the door. I walked over and grabbed it on a hunch.

"Griff, have you gone mad? This is someone's grave." Jess responded to my actions in an angry whisper.

Pulling with all my strength it became apparent that this door had not been opened in a long while. Heaving back with all my weight the door began to inch back, picking up the dirt that had built up in front of it into a little mound. Eventually the door parted enough for us to be able to squeeze through. Standing back as a small dust cloud poured from the top of the door I coughed. Jess pushed her way in front of me and peered into the opening.

"Ladders?!" she exclaimed. "But… how could you know that? Where's the body?"

Regaining my breath from the grasp of the ancient dust, I joined her next to the entrance.

"The black cross on the door, it was on the other two hatches to the tunnels Was just a guess really. If there was a body in here, I would probably have felt pretty bad."

Jess gave the barest hint of a smile. At least it was something, a hint of optimism.

"Common then, let's find Dalton."

Chapter 13

A Common Ritual

Inside the crypt the wooden ladders looked stable enough to scale down. The light from the torch was switched on and attached to the pistol on my belt pointing downwards to guide me past an array of cobwebs. Actually the shaft was not too deep, only about ten feet down at best.

Hitting the floor it was actually soggy compared to the ground in the tunnel before. My feet squelched as I made room for Jess to follow me down. Taking my hand she popped down by my side. I felt quite gentlemanly. The thought was short lived, there was a world to save, or Dalton at the very least.

Spearing off in two directions we walked a couple of feet to the left passage till underneath the church. Actually a set of ladders again appeared lit up by tiny rays of light from above, shining through the cobwebs and dust. A muffled sound of people talking could be heard up ahead as well.

Treading carefully I could see a set of circular holes penetrated the ceiling. Lifting my finger to my lips I indicated to Jess to be quiet. Then scaling the ladders till I was directly under the hatch I spied through.

Ophanim's information seemed to have paid off. Vaguely I could see Dalton – he was alive! Although not in the best of situations he was tied up to a cross underneath a large circular stained glass window showing an image of the sun and the moon. I assumed I must be located directly under the altar.

There was no way of seeing what was going on at ground level from where I was. All I could see was Dalton, an altar and the wooden ceiling surrounded by various frescos painted into the walls. I could hear people conversing amongst themselves but not loud enough to make out anything clearly.

A fully robed man suddenly appeared above me. Luckily he was fully clothed beneath the robe or that really would have ruined my day. The arrow on my device was going crazy pointing at him. He started proclaiming something in Romanian and a unified roar could be heard from the opposite side of the room.

"I really would prefer it if I could just go!" shouted Dalton but he was ignored.

Loud grunts could be heard from across the church. I could see ropes being moved upwards until a huge car-sized glass prism came into sight, which could only mean one thing. A small section of the roof opened up beaming moonlight onto the prism and black tar slowly began to form across the large stained glass window behind Dalton.

"Well, this is rather unnerving," I heard Dalton complain.

"You know that plan of going in gung ho? Well, I think now is the time," I said, looking down at Jess.

"It's about time," she replied handling her pistol.

"This is going to get messy, fast. You get Dalton down and I'll deal with the rest," I warned.

"Get him down?" she quizzed.

"You'll understand as soon as we are in," I replied.

Waiting until the robed man was once again directly above me I aimed my device straight upwards. The portal had already been opened; there was no time to lose. Fire.

Crack, Whistle.

The wooden hatch cracked up above me but even worse was the bone and muscle crumpling and cracking into each other whilst being removed from the centre of the man's body. The man was left in two halves dropping to the floor in a flood of blood which poured through the hatch and onto my face.

I knew there was no time to hesitate or be squeamish. What was important was saving Dalton while still having the element of surprise.

With the electrical charge of the device running through me I had the energy to lift the remains and the hatch upwards allowing me and Jess to jump out and into action.

"Well, I'll be damned!" exclaimed Dalton.

Stone walls and pillars surrounded us. More paintings and tapestries were hung from the front of cubicles around the outside of the aisles. Lots of strange symbols and images I had no knowledge of were on the paintings. A large hole was visible in the centre of the room where the prism once lay. Just of slight concern was the scores of white hooded people sitting in the aisles as still as stone, faces full of shock. The wrist device had no idea which way to point. I was getting déjà vu from the island all over again with this cult in front of me.

Jess had instantly begun working on retrieving Dalton when it all really started to kick off. One of the many possessed people congregated in the pews stood up pointing at me and let out a high pitched gurgling howl. After hearing it so many times it was amazed me how it still drilled right through my spine. More stood up in protest and moved into the centre of the aisles when something stopped them unexpectedly.

From behind me the circular black blob running down the back wall of the church began changing into a new shape. A large bubble was forming for a couple of seconds, inflating until it suddenly burst by the flight of a large flying Remnant swooping through.

Dalton's cross was knocked down onto its side then swung round so that Dalton ended up hitting the floor flat but at a shorter distance. His face scrunched up for a second but he said nothing.

The tar-covered beast continued its flight swooping blindly across the aisles until it was met with a sudden crash against the strung up prism. It swayed side to side, the pulleys mounted up high creaked and blew out dust and small chunks from the stone walls. Wrestling itself free from the ropes the beast latched itself onto the ceiling while the prism lost its mounting.

Brackets tore from the walls and the prism dropped onto a large group of the possessed. It was horrific. Bodies became trapped and wedged under the intense weight of the glass. Limbs were torn off completely while some remained stuck. One man was completely underneath and just dissipated in an explosion of blood whilst another had his lower half trapped causing his upper half to inflame like a tube of toothpaste being rolled. He began bleeding from his eyes and mouth but was still alive.

By now the portal had shut off and the last of the tar was dripping away from the window or hardening. Jess had just finished untying Dalton from the crucifix when the flying Remnant flew across the room and crashed through the large circular window into freedom. Glass and black flakes rained down over our heads. I took shelter under my arm and closed my eyes to stop glass getting in.

"Get a move on, Griff!" Jess screamed from behind me.

Opening my eyes I saw a small swarm of white figures spattered with red dots of blood heading toward me.

"Just fucking try it!" I yelled holding the rifle up to my shoulder.

The ACOG scope zoomed me in slightly and I could see the anger on their faces. Without hesitation I fired a couple rounds into the first man's chest. The weapon was semi-automatic and ripped a hole right through him. He dropped. The wrist device was still charging and I felt like I could get them all. No second thoughts ran through my head, no deep insight into if they were all possessed or that I was shooting people. All I could think was they had to die because I wasn't going to. Bill died because of them and they were going to follow suit.

Quickly changing my target I shot one then another then another. A hand tugged on my shoulder.

"Move it now!" Jess yelled in my ear.

Looking back Dalton had already dropped down the hole and Jess was descending as well. Inching backwards over broken glass I made my way to the hatch. The possessed were closing in; there were just more of them then I had bullets. I didn't even climb down the ladders but just dropped, causing mud to spatter up my legs.

"Time to go," Dalton commanded.

We began running down the dark tunnel. I had switched to my pistol to make use of the torch. Splashing could be heard from behind as the hoard followed. Sprinting further and further down the tunnel the floor became wetter forming a pool around my feet. I had no idea which direction we were heading just that it was away from the possessed.

Dalton who was in the lead stopped abruptly and I almost caved into the back of him.

"Woah! Why'd you stop?" I questioned. He didn't need to answer me as I could see plainly why. In front the tunnel began sloping downwards and was swallowed up by a pool of water blocking the way. It must have happened when I blocked off the water flow at the opposite end of the tunnel system.

"Oh, shit!" I stared wide eyed.

Loud shooting came from behind as Jess began firing at the oncoming possessed. I had an idea all be it not the best I've ever had but it might keep us alive, we'd be dead anyway if the possessed got a hold of us.

Aiming my wrist device up along the left support beam I fired.

Crack, Whistle

It tore a long section of the beam away and it began to creak. Jumping backwards the ground began to shake, the beam snapped under the stress and the ceiling came tumbling down on top of a couple possessed. It had worked – this could give us some precious time if they tried to dig after us.

"What the hell was that? Now what do we do!" Jess screamed at me. Nothing like a bit of appreciation from your fellow survivors to keep you motivated.

"That was me keeping us alive, cheers!" I shouted back. She seemed a little taken aback that I raised my voice at her, probably a bad idea on my part but I was under the charge effects and I kind of lose control when under the influence.

To be completely fair I was covered in mud, dust, blood, black tar and was wet. I had just lost a good friend and learned another guy was a monster and was completely exhausted from the hike to the church while being up so late as well as sprinting away from possessed people – yeah, I was pretty pissed off!

"There is only one way." Dalton pointed toward the submerged tunnel.

Directing my gaze from the murky water to Jess she looked back with a sigh. She was, at the end of the day, a coastguard and most likely the best swimmer out of all of us even if it pained Dalton to admit it.

"Goddamn it." She sighed again and approached the pool of browned water.

"You will have almost zero visibility, your best option would be to stick close to one of the walls and the ceiling," Dalton instructed.

"Mhm." She waded into the water till she was no longer touching the floor. With one hand touching the ceiling her head was just above the waterline.

"Here we go!" She said her farewell before her head disappeared into the abyss and her feet splashed out a torrent of water behind her.

I turned my attention to Dalton.

"So we wait?" I asked my rhetorical question.

"Seems so. I must say I was rather surprised to see you both come to my aid. It was quite the dramatic entrance you made. I'm very grateful."

"Well, you know, if you're gonna rescue someone you might as well make a meal of it," I answered whilst focusing on the last few ripples of water dispersing from the pool.

"Although I must enquire of the whereabouts of Ophanim and Mr Greaves?"

"Bill…. didn't make it," I mumbled.

"Oh dear, my deepest sympathies, Mr Holster" He patted my shoulder in emotional consolation.

"It was Ophanim's fault. He closed the portal on him. The Remnant got out of his dungeon and freed that Lucian bloke who must have opened the portal and let a load of them out. We managed to kill them all but Bill got dragged into the portal and Ophanim… just closed it on him… Lucian also got away. Not only that but me and Jess found out that he's been experimenting on the locals to try and find out who's possessed. It was sick, Dalton, you don't want to see the shit he's been doing. Jess shot the bastard in the leg and locked him in one of his crycells," I explained.

"My God. Seems the situation has been getting out of hand."

"Yeah, definitely," I replied. I was becoming worried as Jess had been gone a while now. I was no breath holding champion but I know if she had not made it by now then she must be very close to drowning.

"I've lost too much, Dalton." I continued to stare at the point where Jess had disappeared.

"We have all lost too much, Mr Holster," he replied. His cheery attitude seemed to have left him. Perhaps there was a little more to this man than I had originally thought, he certainly seemed more human right now than when I first met him.

Our conversation was cut short as the top layer of the pool began bubbling, followed by a gasping Jess bursting through. We helped her out of the murky water as she caught her breath.

"Follow the top right corner and you'll get to an air pocket, there's a ladder that goes to a wooden door," she told us.

"May I have use of your light, Mr Holster," Dalton enquired wading into the water and disappearing within seconds.

"Go on then, Griff, I need to catch my breath again," Jess signalled.

Steadily I sifted through the water till I was about waist deep. I had never been a strong swimmer. Had Jasper not rescued me from the plane crash at the island I possibly might not have been here at all.

Now neck deep I had my hands on the ceiling and wall and my last sight was of Jess resting on her knees breathing heavily. Taking three large breaths I closed up my lungs and dove backwards under the water. Without daring to open my eyes I made my way, exerting air from my nostrils at a fixed rate while kicking out with my feet. Small particles of dirt hit my face as I swam, each time giving me a slight shock as I had no idea where I was heading.

Oxygen began rapidly running low, I could feel my lungs painfully attempting to collect every last scrap available. Starting to panic I found myself clawing the walls and pulling myself hard to make the distance. Luckily while trying to dig my hand into the ceiling I was met with nothing and ended up floating upwards and out of the deep.

Popping into existence I engaged in swallowing a mass amount of air whilst feeling blindly around for some ladders.

"Get yourself up here." I heard Dalton's voice from above. "You must make some space for Jess," he instructed.

Wiping the muck from my face I saw the ladders with blurred vision and scaled up them till I was just under Dalton who was showing the way with his torch. Jess soon appeared after and followed up the ladders behind me.

We were all freezing wet and lost with no idea where we would come out. There could be an ambush waiting at the top – maybe these tunnels were not as secret as I first thought.

"Well, let us see what's in store for us here," Dalton said as he pushed the hatch up above him.

Chapter 14

Teutonic Knights

Rescuing Dalton brought me a little happiness in a rather grim situation where everything had taken a turn for the worse. Bill was dead, Ophanim was a demented psychopath, half the village were possessed and out to catch us and now there was a flying Remnant on the loose. Everything was just peachy. We could just fly away and I could blow up the capsule device and take out all the possessed but this seemed far too heartless as I knew there were still normal people alive in the area. Of course, I knew if the situation became unsalvageable it may be the only option remaining but I refused to think that was the case right now, however glum it might seem.

Light burst down into the hole we were in and Dalton escaped up out of the flooded damp tunnel. I followed him and ended up in a warm bright room.

There were blades and blunt weapons mounted on the walls and full suits of knights' armour stood upright looking directly at us. The light in the windowless room was coming from an open fireplace and a couple of wall mounted oil lamps. The walls themselves were white and covered in old maps; wooden beams held the walls and ceiling in place using the more tradition style of building methods. Wooden stairs led up one side to a large wood and iron door which must be the exit.

Most surprisingly though was the large engraved wooden table next to the stairs which was occupied by no less than ten men and women dressed in everyday civilian clothes, staring at us with a look of disbelief shared by Dalton and myself and of course Jess as she joined the group from the dark below. To be fair, out of both groups I would suspect they were the more surprised to see three strangers soaked to the bone and armed with guns popping up in the middle of their meeting.

Then I noticed that two of the congregated people sitting at the table were no other than the couple who had helped me escape previously in the night. What a coincidence.

"Sorry to disturb you, we seemed to have made a wrong turn. If you would be so kind as to show us out that would be excellent," Dalton asked in his usual comical fashion.

Head of the table was a large muscular man with black hair, brown eyes and facial hair hiding most of his face. He stood up and walked over to us in large strides, looking rather bemused at his unwelcome guests.

"How did you find us?" he demanded with a heavy loud voice.

I was still intrigued by the fact we had not yet been threatened or attacked. Not a single weapon was produced and we were well outnumbered although heavily armed in comparison.

"Those two people there showed me this tunnel with a black cross on it and we found another cross in the church and it led us here. It's a bit flooded down there by the way," I explained unnecessarily whilst dripping water all over the floor.

The large man's expression turned more concerned.

"That is the cross of the order of Teutonic knights." He pulled a small black cross emblem hanging on some string around his neck, from beneath his collar.

"Why were you at the church? That place is not safe," he questioned.

"The Remnant took Dalton there and we had to save him," Jess pointed out.

"You know of the possessed then?" he asked again looking to Jess.

"We know of them alright, we've been running from them, killing them, breaking their stuff. Just all round pissing them off really," I told them.

"You were not followed?"

"No we collapsed the tunnel behind us and made sure we could not be followed," Dalton answered.

I was trying to concentrate but I was cold and wet and drawn to the fire by necessity. The large burley gentleman returned to the table, spoke some words of Romanian to one of the group who then proceeded to climb the stairs.

"It must have been you who caused the warning bell to alarm earlier. You have done well to get away, even with the help of Dumitru and Ileana." He pointed at the couple who had helped me escape.

"Yeah, thanks for that by the way." I expressed my gratitude to the couple who gave a slight smile and Dumitru raised his hand as if to say it was no problem.

"I myself am Christian and this is the last of the Teutonic knights."

Just then the man who had been sent away returned with three sets of robes and gave them straight to us. He then pulled three seats over to the fire and gestured for us to sit.

Christian pulled a seat over and joined us by the fire as the rest of his group continued their conversation.

"Teutonic order, they are German if I am not mistaken?" Dalton enquired with a little pride in his tone.

"That is right. The order was sent over in the thirteenth century. People were told they had been sent to protect the west from barbarians and although this is partly true the main objective was to find and destroy the supernatural which were rumoured to be in the area: vampires, werewolves, witches, demons and gargoyles. The order was great. They had fortified over two hundred churches in the area as we thought God would protect us from this evil. We now know of course that this was not the case and all these monsters come from these 'Remnant' as you call them. We have been fighting a silent war against these demonic creatures for centuries and now, only a handful of us remain to fight on in this silent war."

Damn, and I thought I had it tough spending a couple of days with these monsters whereas these people had spent their entire lives hiding and fighting them. I felt a little ashamed now.

"It is only the three of you here? What is it you seek anyway?" Christian asked curiously.

"Well, I do not know of what level of information you have on the Remnant, but I assume you know of the portals," Dalton said.

"Ah yes, the gateways. We have seen them."

"Well the original gateways as you call them are opened by great machines. We are here to destroy these machines and to stop the Remnant from arriving here for good; this machine just so happens to be under the castle. There were four of us but sadly one did not make it and we were also accompanied by the man known as Dracula, you may have heard of him?"

Christian changed his attitude at the sound of Dracula's name. "Why would you be in the presence of that man? He is evil and has scourged this land for years. His life must be ended at first opportunity before he has the chance to take more of us."

A little late now for the damage had already been done.

"We have him trapped in the castle in his secret underground lair. We could help each other as we obviously want the same thing – to get rid of all the Remnant," I suggested.

"That would be of great help to us, we must destroy him at once. Too many times he has snatched members of our group and the community for his own gain. We thought he was part of the possessed but there is something different about him which we do not understand. We only know he must be dealt with," Christian explained. "But how did you find him? We have searched many a time in Bran Castle. And why would he not have killed you? This I do not understand."

Pulling the sleeve up from the robe and my jacket I revealed my wrist device sitting squarely on my arm, gleaming in the flickering light of the fire. Leaning in closely Christian curiously studied the object.

"This lets me see if someone is possessed or not and points to the closest Remnant. It also shoots a beasty gravity beam that just fucks up anything in the way. This is why he used us so he could use this thing without him getting in danger while testing it."

"Then his downfall is underestimating you, and that is our gain." Christian smiled relaxing back into his chair.

My clothes were drying nicely and I was beginning to feel rather sleepy lazing by the fire. It was nice to have a breather although it could have been under better circumstances that was for sure. Jess was already half asleep in her chair and Dalton was continuing the conversation with Christian obviously extremely interested in the order's history although never giving away the fact that he was part of a different group who had the same agenda. Before I knew it I had drifted off, despite my best efforts to stay awake and listen to the conversation. It felt rude to fall asleep in front of company but at the end of the day it could not be helped as my body had crashed.

Dreaming was once again as vivid as ever, uncontrollable and far too realistic to react in any other than an instinctive way. Sprinting through the dark catacombs below Bran I could hear Jasper's voice calling for me from ever changing directions. I had no idea which way to run but that is all I did, run, trying to find him. Stumbling down one passage with my pistol held up the torch revealed a trail of water running toward me. Jasper's voice became louder, calling for help.

At full sprint I came to a flooded tunnel and caught the end of a hand being pulled below the surface. I wouldn't let them take him from me. I dove head first into the pool, my torch shining a beam through the murky water where Jasper's helpless face was being pulled away from mine. Something tugged me from behind. I turned and saw a Remnant beast pulling itself along the floor through the water behind me. I gasped and bubbles erupted over my eyes and I swam as hard as I could after Jasper who had disappeared.

The Remnant never caught me and I burst through to the other side of the pool but Jasper was nowhere in sight. Without hesitation, for the beast was behind me, I sprinted down the blackened tunnels. That's when I began to hear Bill's voice calling for me through the darkness. Turning a corner I saw him being dragged by two enormous Remnant beasts, both drooling onto the floor as their claws dug hard into Bill's shoulders impaling him.

Attempting to shoot them didn't even make them flinch and they walked into a tar portal at the end of a tunnel. I sprinted after them as Bill's outstretched hand reached for mine but, as I attempted to grab hold, I hit the wall full force, as the portal had disappeared and with it, Bill.

Slumped against the wall I despaired – I had let two people be taken from me already. I heard the shrieks of the Remnant cries and around the corner came a hoard of possessed led by Lucian. Behind me the wall had transformed into a tunnel and I picked myself up hurriedly and ran.

The sound of footsteps and the roar of the possessed came ever closer. Flame torch lights flickered in all directions and I had nowhere else to run; I was surrounded there was no escape. Shooting wildly into a crowd of demented faces I dropped a couple of them but no matter how many I shot, there were always more. They were on me, I was had. Turning to one side I was met by Ophanim whose face was malicious. He grabbed my neck with one hand and thrust his sword into my chest with the other. Breathless and wide eyed I stared into his cold eyes, my chest feeling extremely tight.

I woke up in a fit of coughing trying frantically to breathe.

Chapter 15

Recovery

Jess was sitting next to me holding my shoulder as I woke up. She comforted me back into reality as my breathing returned to normal.

"Nightmares again?"

"Yeah, it's alright, just dreams" I replied. She gave me a stern look but did not argue.

"How long was I out?" I enquired whilst rubbing my chest.

"Well it's the afternoon now so quite a while… lazy sod."

I laughed still rubbing my chest where the imaginary sword had pierced me.

Still in the basement room I had fallen asleep for hours in my chair next to the fire. The room was now completely empty bar Jess and myself.

"Where are the others?"

"They all went back home at day break. Dalton and Christian went upstairs and kept on chatting and I stayed and slept next to you but you must have needed it way more than me cause I've been awake a while now," she explained.

Sweat was on my forehead which I wiped onto the sleeve of the gown. The rest of my clothes had dried up whilst being heated in front of the fire which was now whittled down to a smouldering pile of ashes.

"Think I want to get upstairs myself."

Jess looked as eager as myself to leave the secretive meeting room. "Good idea," she said lifting herself up.

Together we wandered up the wooden staircase and I pushed open the large door with relative ease. Natural light shone through the crack and was blinding as it hit my face. I covered my sight with one hand. I was in the hallway of a very ordinary looking house with a couple of doorways, a set of stairs leading up another level and an entrance at the end with a blurred window letting in the daylight. Décor was extremely bland with brown walls and a small wooden table with a single vase holding a small bunch of flowers. I didn't expect much in the way of decoration as I assumed the country was poor, although the decorative instruments of war in the basement may have proven me otherwise.

As if on cue Dalton popped his head around the corner of one of the rooms.

"Ah, glad you have joined the realm of the living. Mr Holster. Why don't you join us?"

His room contained another fireplace, some basic brown sofas and chairs to accompany the terrible walls and shelves. The only modern technology present was a radio and an old square box television – it was like travelling ten years into the past. Christian was sitting in an armchair by the fire with Dalton opposite him. Jess and I parked ourselves on the couch. Most notably odd was the window facing out into a street which saw life go on as usual, no monsters, no possessed people, no horrible fog – it was just a normal day very reminiscent of looking out of the hospital window back in England.

Dalton must have noticed the confused look on my face and aptly intervened.

"Strange isn't it? How life can go on oblivious to the goings on of the Remnant," Dalton said.

"Mmm, yeah it's strange alright. Why isn't there a flying Remnant massacring everyone? And how come nobody cares about all the noise last night?" I enquired very confused.

This time it was Christian's turn to explain. He leaned forward in his chair which creaked on the wooden floor under his immense size.

"Over the years we have learned that the demons hunt at night when they can use the darkness. During the day they hide and wait like bats. The possessed do the same, acting normal to bring no attention on themselves, a kind of social camouflage. The locals see no difference in them and know no better and, because we cannot tell who is and is not one of them, we cannot trust anyone other than our group. We know none of us are possessed as we stay together and if it were so then we would have been overrun a long time ago. That is another reason we use the ancient tunnels to travel at night unseen. Think of daylight as a time of truce – neither of our groups wants to bring attention to what is really happening here. As for the night, the locals are extremely superstitious. They believe the large crowds are hunting the paranormal when in fact they do the complete opposite. People are easily frightened and persuaded to stay indoors and close windows during the night which, in fact, is for the best." His explanation made the situation quite a bit clearer.

As I watched out the window crowds of people wandered by. My wrist device acted up every now and again pointing at certain individuals mingling with the crowds as if everything were normal. One of the men my device pointed out was even smoking a cigarette. Was it for show or did it actually enjoy it? I suppose it didn't have to worry about getting cancer or having its lungs seize up.

"This is mad," I said in disbelief. "Surely the police would do something though?"

"They are probably compromised. As soon as anything were to get out of hand, I believe the possessed would kill the rest."

"What about the Remnant though? We can't just let it fly about and kill people at night," Jess said.

"The dragon demon you mean? Yes, we have our means of dealing with those. You forget this is not our first time in dealing with these beasts. All will become clear at night where you will help us rid the demonic dragon and we together can then rid this place of Dracula and the rest of the possessed!" Christian exclaimed excitedly.

Seeing him so excited made me imagine him as a kind of polarised santa, big and jolly as well as being a demon killer.

"So, what do we do till then?" I asked.

"You could go out and explore. It will be safe as the demons do not like to draw attention on themselves in daylight. Also you are welcome to stay and look around the house; it will only be a couple hours till dark falls," Christian suggested.

A couple of hours… I must really have slept for some time again. I suppose becoming nocturnal is natural for this kind of ordeal.

"I think I might just stay inside for now. I've had enough crazy shit for the time being and could use some time off my feet."

"Think that sounds pretty good to me too," Jess agreed.

"Suit yourselves, I must ready the supplies for tonight. I shall return before dark, meanwhile, make yourselves at home," instructed Christian before getting out of his seat and making his way to the front door.

"If it is all well and good with the two of you, I think I will stay here and indulge myself in some literature," Dalton said whilst browsing a selection of antiquarian books.

With that Jess and I left the room to have a little look around. The house was normal in every conceivable way, bathroom, bedroom and kitchen. We did take an assortment of food from the kitchen and devoured it in record time; I believe any mice would go starving with the lack of crumbs left over. My stomach's rumbling subsided for good after that.

Stopping off in the bathroom I privileged myself to the first shower in days. Being an avid runner in the mornings I always knew the importance of showering and hygiene as well as having the satisfying sensation of having dirt run off, knowing I have earned the right to rest afterwards.

The final room to inspect was upstairs at the very end of the hallway. Inside, walls were covered in photographs, news articles and a map of the area covered in drawing pins. Pictures of Dracula were visible as well as other people who I presume were possessed or at least suspected of being possessed. A key on the bottom right of the map showed the representation of the pins – red for possessed, blue for human and green for unknown. The amount of red and green on the board did not reassure.

"Wow, obsess much?" Jess said entering the room behind me.

"Well at least he's thorough."

There was a large wooden workbench with a huge book open on it. Sifting through the pages I saw many hand drawn ideas for traps, and maps of the area covered in plans. It was clear that this Christian fellow took what he did extremely seriously and paid attention to every necessary detail. He seemed to know exactly how dangerous Remnant were and took every precaution to plan every move meticulously. Thinking about it properly I guess you don't grow old while fighting an army of Remnant unless you know exactly what you are up against and what you are doing. I was actually impressed with the level of commitment present and don't think I could ever produce the concentration levels necessary for such commitment.

One of the wall charts showed the vast maze of underground tunnels with entrances at many different points. Red was coloured into one section of the tunnel system near the church and under a house. I imagine that would be the section I personally compromised with a torrent of water, I should really apologise for that next time I see Christian.

Jess had her back to me shuffling through layers of papers stuck to the wall. She stopped and examined a photo of Ophanim. Seeing the pictures of Ophanim made me think of Bill again.

"Sorry I couldn't save him Jess… I tried my best," I said softly. She did not turn around but remained still with her hand on the wall.

"It wasn't your fault, Griff, he would have known that," she replied with the same soft tone.

"Maybe… I just think he trusted the wrong person," I said.

"Who? Ophanim?" she asked confused and turning around.

"No. Me," I replied becoming self-conscious of my failures.

Gently she took my hand and looked me in the eyes. It seemed the comforting had taken a complete role reversal from being in the woods before.

"Griff, back in the hospital while we waited for you to recover he told me what he thought of you. He said he could see you were still growing, naïve, prone to mistakes even."

I didn't know how this was meant to make me feel any better, hopefully she would not seek a career in inspirational speech making after this was all over.

"But," she continued, "he could see that you were a good person which is what made him trust you from the start. He said that is what made you slow to make decisions; trying to judge the best outcome, letting your brain and conscience loose. He realised you were not a trained killer like him and he admired how you handled yourself in the situation we were in. Believe me, he doesn't say this kind of thing about just anyone," she informed me.

"Thanks. I still wish I could have saved him, though," I whispered cracking a brief smile.

"I know, Griff, but this is the life we have now. Someone's gotta live it," she explained.

"Yeah, I wouldn't want anyone else to feel this kind of crap."

We completed our browse of the room and returned to Dalton downstairs.

"Feed your curiosity sufficiently," he asked without removing his face from the page as if using some sixth sense to know we were there.

"You could say that. This bloke seems to be extremely organised," I said.

Dalton lowered the book to look at us. "Organised to a wonderful standard. If there is one thing I love, it is efficiency, it is in my blood as a German! And these people seem to be outstanding at what they do and, with such limited resources and headcount, it is quite admirable. I imagine they will be of much use to us, or perhaps I should say, we will be much use to one another."

Sitting ourselves next to Dalton I rested my eyes again, although this time merely conserving my energy. I had a feeling I would need it all tonight. Twisting the dial on the radio Jess turned on the local station. It was playing some weird gypsy folk music which I can't say was exactly my taste but it was nice to hear something a bit more uplifting.

Chapter 16

Old Techniques

Few hours passed and the sun began to set. I was in a foreign land attempting to save the world, or at least part of the world, from creatures of a long lost past with an assortment of weird and wonderful people. My life really was more fucked up than I could ever could have imagined, but I kind of enjoyed it, except for the deaths of friends which brought a huge downer on the whole thing. Maybe I'm sounding a little too light hearted about the whole ordeal, I was in all honesty devastated and definitely scared, believe you me. I think it's just the fact that there is so much happening for my brain to completely register and assign the correct emotions at the correct time. I'm sure when this is all over I'll probably break down in tears and need therapy or end up in a lunatic asylum but, until then, I just had to deal with it all.

Christian turned up as the skies began to darken. I was watching out the window as the last of the people exited the streets and retreated back to their respective homes, obeying the unwritten curfew.

Slouched in the couch feeling fatigued and lazy I couldn't be bothered to get my voice to react to his entrance. Luckily Dalton was there to speak for us.

"Everything prepared I presume?"

"All is ready. If you would come with me we must use a different tunnel entrance before total dark is upon us."

"Haway then!" I lifted myself out of my seated position against my body's will.

Rummaging around behind the couch Christian grabbed hold of a sheathed sword that was hidden inside a secret compartment. He smiled as he pulled the blade out slightly to inspect its condition.

"Really? More swords? Don't you think it's a bit outdated? I mean, a possessed could easily have a gun and shoot you dead on the spot," I reasoned.

Christian continued to smile and, pointing the sword straight, he pushed his index finger into a small hole in the handle. A second later a gunshot erupted from the hilt of the sword firing a bullet into the fireplace. Smoke residue plumed from the hilt along the blade. Christian pressed another button and a cartridge of ammunition dropped from the handle which he instantly pushed back in.

"Do not worry, we are prepared," he assured.

Quite impressive! I had to admit that having a gun sword is something that would come in extremely useful. It seemed obvious to have only small caliber rounds as you can fit more in the handle whilst keeping it lightweight as well as preventing any unnecessary self-harm with the effects of heavy recoil.

I nodded my head in approval.

Gathering outside the door in our small group we waited as Christian locked the building behind us for the night. Reluctantly I had traded weapons with Dalton so that I was once more in possession of the pistol and he had the much deadlier rifle.

"Follow me everyone," he commanded. We went as a group down a cobbled pathway, in the opposite direction to the church until we came across another house. Christian knocked at the door and we were welcomed in by one of the men I recognised from the meeting the night before.

Accompanied by a couple more of the group we went into the tunnel system via a hatch located in the cellar of the man's house. From there we walked for about fifteen minutes down the blackened damp tunnels until we came across another set of ladders. Up the top and out in the open we were located next to a large flowing river, each side covered in trees and undergrowth hiding it from the village.

Travelling slightly further down the river I could see ropes dangling from stray dead trees. On closer inspection I could see the ropes were hidden in small trenches leading to the river. On our side was a small barge with a metal top roughly six feet squared in size and held to a tree by rope that stretched to the opposing side of the river where it was tied to another tree. Stacks of chopped up wooden logs lay in a pile next to the barge. It seemed highly elaborate whatever it was.

Appearing on the other side of the river the remaining members of the knights grabbed a rope tied to a tree, as did the group on our side. Heaving the rope attached to a pulley system hidden up in the trees caused the tension to increase, eventually raising the rope from the river. From beneath the water's surface emerged a large reinforced metallic domed cage with hundreds of spiked points facing inwards much like the cruel iron maiden used for torture only larger and with a hollow bottom.

After being hoisted up till a good fifteen foot gap separated the cage from the river, Christian proceeded to tie the ends of the rope around a hook attached to a thick tree. The cage was poised and ready.

Two of the group stacked the wooden logs onto the makeshift raft before sticking a bunch of newspaper into the centre of the mound.

"Ways to take care of the demons has been passed down from generations, they seek the flame and in doing so fall into our trap," Christian explained.

Over the mountains the glow from the sun was practically completely out of sight and darkness had spread over the tree canopies. Christian walked to the barge and set the paper inside on fire. The flames rippled and grew inside until a steady light ate into the darkness. Tugging on the rope on the opposite side the barge was pulled underneath the cage and the snare was obvious, like a giant bird trap. I remembered our plan on the island to lure the flying Remnant by setting fire to the hotel, although this was way more thought out.

Much to my surprise Christian managed to open up the trunk of the tree that the pulleys were deployed on. The seemingly hollow tree contained long spears that he threw onto the floor facing the river.

"Now you get inside," Christian instructed pointing to the next tree. On the opposite side of the water the others had also thrown numerous spears to the floor and entered the hollow trees. Closely inspecting one of the trees I found it was hinged and had a small carved handle to pull open. Placing myself inside I shut the bark door and was able to see out of a small slit cut in just at eye level. Everyone else had entered their respective trees and lay in wait.

Christian poked his hand out of one of the holes in his tree next to the rope that held the cage suspended in position, he gave the bilingual signal of a thumbs up and retracted his arm.

Blackness swept over the sky with only the river and embankments illuminated by the raging fire. Everything was still and quiet outside apart from the crackling of the wood being engulfed in flame.

A swooping noise echoed in the distant skies that became louder with every passing second. The noise quickened as if the monster was slowing down and steadying itself by flapping its wings violently forwards. Then, my tree shook. It had perched itself right above me. Loud bloodcurdling screeches came from above followed by snarling and gargling while my hiding place shook further. It was moving down the tree. My heart was in overdrive whereas my breath was not functioning at all.

Talons penetrated the surface of the tree trunk directly next to my face. I stared down at the sharp claw just an inch away from cutting into me. Just one of the talons was the size of my full hand. I pushed myself back as far as I could against the other side of the hollow. Various body parts glanced past the viewing slit as the claws dug further and further down the tree. The strong stench of sulphur filled my small safe house.

It descended onto the floor and stood on its hind legs with its wings spanned. It remained in place surveying the area and inspecting the flames with curiosity.

Daringly I forced my back from the hollow and perched my face against the viewing slit with the cold bark spiking against my forehead. I regulated my breathing keeping it quiet and as slow as possible.

Standing directly in front of the flame the Remnant's body was completely black, hiding all distinctive features. It was a large shadow blending in with the night engulfing all the fire for itself. Its body flicked out of existence for a brief second allowing the light of the fire to flash my eyes before the apparition returned. Lurking toward the river bed it sniffed the flowing waters intrigued and I felt myself becoming impatient. For the first time I felt an excitement, for the hunt, for once not to be the prey.

With a couple of strong downward thrusts with its wings the monstrosity hovered above the ground. I could feel the force of the winds blow through the slit in the tree and had to blink a couple of times to get the dirt out of my eyes. The beast proceeded to glide across the river until it landed upon the barge surrounding the flames with its wings and hugging the fire close to its body.

That was it! I spied over to Christian's tree to see a hand slowly advance from the hole and grab a firm hold of the rope suspending the cage. On the opposite side of the river one of the other members was repeating the movements. Timing had to be perfect. Christian's other hand came out and counted down the fingers to make sure the ropes were pulled in unison.

Five... Four... Three... Two... One!

Zipping through the pulleys at some velocity, the ropes ascended into the trees as the metal cage fell from the sky landing smack bang on top of the creature. It screeched loudly and thrashed about chaotically trying its best to escape as the cage dug down into the riverbed half submerging the beast.

Christian and the other members of the knights burst out of the trees grabbing the spears from the floor and quickly jabbed them into the Remnant. Sounds turned from high pitched screeches to fluid filled gurgling and groans. With one final blow one of the spears had pierced the beast's heart causing it to slouch against the side of the cage one arm reaching out.

The last of the Remnants remains evaporated into the wind. The Teutonic knights did not dawdle but raised the cage, pulled the barge to one side and re-lowered the cage into the water.

"That is how you take care of the dragon demons." Christian smiled showing no signs of fatigue. To him this was everyday life and nothing out of the ordinary.

"Very good show. Simplicity at its best really." Dalton clapped his hands in enjoyment.

"Good, but we are not finished. There is much to be done. Take us to Dracula and we will end his evil ways for good," Christian said.

"I don't mind that at all, the man is sick in the fucking head," I replied.

What little sympathy I once had for Ophanim had completely vanished to be replaced by a strong hatred. The Angious may be stronger and more intelligent than humans but living in isolation for centuries could break any mind.

"I concur, although it would be wise of us to gather as much information as possible from him. We must think of the bigger picture. He spent years committed to researching the possessed and the portals and while I do not condone his methods in the slightest, we should not waste his knowledge, otherwise those people will have died in vain," Dalton pointed out.

"Very well, so be it. As long as you allow me the satisfaction of driving my sword through his evil heart," Christian said with a smirk.

He turned toward the tunnel entrance and we were off once again, this time, to finish Ophanim for good and finally finish what we came here to do.

Chapter 17

Deal with a Devil

It was nice to have a large group accompany us for once, I felt more secure now. Knowing exactly what the plan was proved a great boost to moral. My life had some direction and protection which was a relief from the usual struggle for survival I had grown so accustom to in the past week. Bill's death still haunted me, as did Jasper's, but my mind was focused completely on the mission at hand – retrieve the information, kill Ophanim and destroy the capsule device. Easy.

Water flowed down the tunnel from up ahead and we were forced to stick close to the sides to prevent ourselves sliding back down. I recognised some of the symbols from my previous excursion through the catacomb system.

Out in the open fresh air once more we gathered at the base of Bran Castle out of sight from any spying Remnant. Sneaking our way up we managed to reach the front entrance without any hindrance. It was all far too easy so far. Christian gave commands for some of his men to remain at the entrance on watch duty. Inside the castle grounds his men spread out and assumed various positions, it was clear they had been here before.

With the rest of the group on guard duty only Dalton, Jess, Christian, two knights and I remained to go down into the secret chamber where Ophanim was imprisoned. One press of the button under the old piano and the passageway was opened. Christian seemed to be beaming in delight, finally being able to find the foe who had evaded him his entire life.

"You are mine now," he muttered as he led the group down the stone staircase.

Shivers ran down my spine as I was about to enter the chamber, the classic notion of things going too smooth for comfort crossed my mind. My intuition proved to be correct as the cage at the end of the room was empty. Ophanim was nowhere to be seen.

We cautiously wandered to the centre console in the room.

"Where is he? You said he was trapped!" Christian turned to us in anger.

"He was right here I swear!" I yelled anxiously.

A sharp screech of bars raising from the ground came from behind, followed by a uniformed tap of footsteps.

"Because, my friends, I did not get out alone!" Ophanim blocked the exit with the erected bars and standing next to him was Lucian baring a large axe, smiling sadistically.

"Yes, it seems we found some common ground when it came to survival. Together with the likes of you trying to stop us, it did not take a lot of convincing for Ophanim to join us," Lucian explained with a menacing grin.

The surrounding doors all opened at once with possessed cult members taking up positions around us holding various medieval looking weapons.

"Not good." I flicked my head back and forth inspecting what we were up against. Outnumbered three to one our chances seemed dire. Even so, I wasn't just going to succumb to fear and allow them the satisfaction of a simple kill. No, I'm not going to stand here and die so easily. My blood was beginning to boil and I felt my hand shaking not in fear of death but of anger and anticipation.

"Now you can all join with the rest of us… or die, it's a simple decisi–"
Crack, Whistle!

Lucian's speech was cut short as I fired the device clipping his shoulder, contorting bone and flesh until his left arm hung precariously from his clothes by a thread. He wailed in surprise – that was my answer to his unfinished question.

Using the charge running through my veins I found target acquisition came naturally as I continued my surprise attack with a barrage of handgun fire. The rest of the group followed suit and began firing into the circle of people. Lucian was peppered with bullets and fell to the floor in a bloody heap. One of the shots must have struck his heart as the Remnant energy left his corpse. Ophanim meanwhile managed to avoid the incoming fire by dodging behind a pillar with a noticeable limp.

A handful of the possessed were instantly killed in the initial confusion and a couple more fell injured; the rest gathered themselves and ran at us. Christian kicked one of the wooden tables at three of the oncoming enemy. Two were thrown back by the force but one flipped over the top landing by Christian's feet. He drove his sword deep into the man's chest and twisted it up and out so that the blade pointed at another oncoming figure who he proceeded to shoot before recovering his stance and slicing the victim diagonally in half.

"Ha ha ha, I love a good fight!" he yelled in the heat of the moment.

Having to defend ourselves from all angles we were forced to spread out across the room. Metallic scraping and smashing sounded across the room as all manner of weapons collided. One of the knights deflected an attack from a mace and bashed the attacker in the face with the hilt of his sword before decapitating him.

Taking cover behind a pillar I fired a few rounds at some cultists closing in behind Dalton who turned and finished them off with his rifle. Strafing around the room to the next pillar I was fairly close to the entrance blocked by the frozen bars. The second knight was ahead of me in a fight with a cultist who he dispatched with ease but was immediately ambushed by another. Shoulder barging the knight into a pillar knocked him off balance and the cultist swung a flail around bashing it into the knight's skull, concaving it against the pillar in an awful crunch. His body slumped to the floor in a heap.

While the cultist was distracted I felt my legs taking control and sprinted toward him. He turned just in time to see me jump double footed into his abdomen causing him to stumble back into the cryobars. Within a second the cultist froze in position with a shocked look on his face.

Falling flat with a crunch my elbow painfully bashed the floor. Directly next to me was the caved in face of the knight, bone extruding the skin. Distracted by the violent image another cultist managed to gain ground on me. A heavy looking mace came flying down at my face but I managed to roll to the side before the weapon removed a chunk of stone from the solid floor.

Under the hood of the attacker was a normal looking middle-aged woman with black hair, hazel eyes and wearing a sadistic smile. Managing to jump up from the floor the woman regained her posture and swung wildly at me again.

The blue lights on my device were still flashing and I fired uncontrollably into her chest with my pistol. She looked in pain from the initial impact of the shots yet recovered instantly and continued her attack with anger in her eyes.

Hectically looking around for a way to get out of my dilemma I spotted the flail on the floor as I backed up close to the cryobars. Tossing my gun to one side I snatched the flail from the floor. Rotating it in the air I side stepped around the woman who had blood running from the wounds in her chest. She swung at me viciously but I managed to deflect her attack with a loud clang. My charge had completed on my device causing my reflexes to slow and because of this the woman recovered and hit me just above the waist. I let out a whimper of pain, but I was lucky it had only been a partial swing and hit the side of me.

Wincing I held the wound with my hand which quickly became covered in blood. The lights disappeared from my device. With the mace lifted above her I took quick aim. Fire.

As the weapon came down the device tore away at her shoulder removing her arm from her body. The mace fell directly down into the gravity shot and basically vanished into thin air before it even hit the ground.

She looked at her missing arm and then at me with ravage crazed eyes. I launched the flail full force at her knees and she crumpled to the floor as her legs gave way. With the newly formed charge running through me I let go of my wound, grabbed the flail from the floor and with both hands I bludgeoned the cultist's chest.

Blood spatter covered my face and large puffs of condensing breath emitted from my mouth as I staggered back against the pillar with bodies lying all around me. I grabbed my injured side once more while inspecting the scene. Everyone was still fighting all around the room. It was chaos.

I watched as Christian and Ophanim exchanged blows in a fast paced fencing match. Ophanim managed to parry one of Christian's attacks and sliced him across the chest. Christian collapsed to the floor panting and wide eyed.

Hastily I picked up my pistol and reloaded as fast as possible, before Ophanim had the chance to deal the final blow. I shot at him only hitting him once in the arm and once in the abdomen but it was enough to avert his attention.

He marched intently toward me with his hindering limp and I panicked. I tried shooting again but I was out of ammunition. My device was charging and the flail was on the floor out of arms' reach. I attempted a punch but he dodged it and, grabbing my neck, he slammed me against the pillar holding me a foot off the floor.

"You could have helped me. We could have all survived but you had me resort to this!" he screamed at my face covering me in spittle.

"You're a fuckin mad man." I coughed trying to claw his hand from my neck.

"Life is all about survival! I am not mad for wishing to survive! Something you have failed to learn! Wheels have already been set in motion beyond my control. The master capsule will soon be activated and all I can do is try to stay alive."

"What are you talking about?" I wheezed through his tight grip.

"The master device controls the signal relay between all other capsules. Once activated, the world will be flooded with Remnant and Angious alike. We are powerless to stop it now."

"So you gave up and turned on us…. you coward." I grimaced as he looked in disgust at me and pulled back his sword hand.

With that I thought my life would end. Much to my surprise Ophanim's expression randomly changed from insane killer to lost soul. He peered downward to the tip of a sword piercing his chest.

"Survive that, bastard," Christian grunted from behind Ophanim.

"No… No!" Ophanim dropped me and I fell on my behind still propped up against the pillar.

Dropping to his knees, Ophanim grabbed the end of the sword extruding from his chest and let out a few deep breaths before turning to stare directly at me. A volley of gunshots rung in my ears as they pierced

Ophanim's back and exited his chest. His eyes became vacant and he slouched in his position then fell to the side. This time a blue mist emitted from his body instead of a red one. He was gone.

Holding my side and struggling to regain breath I turned to look at Christian who had dragged himself along the floor toward me. He pulled himself up against me on the pillar.

"I've waited a long time for this moment. You must not let any of these demons escape this place, Griffin, no matter what. None must survive."

I nodded. "You're gonna be alright though." I tried to reassure him in a very unconvincing tone – I did not believe my own words.

"I will be soon," he said softly as we watched the fighting in the room. Only two cultists remained and were quickly dispatched by the knight and Dalton. It was a miracle that we had survived, the ones of us that had anyway as I looked at the unmoving body of the knight next to me.

Jess let out a loud cry as she noticed the two of us sitting against the pillar with the dead knight close by. I noticed blood running down her arm.

"Are you alright, Jess?" I asked worriedly whilst remaining sat next to Christian.

"Am I alright? Of course, Griff, look at yourself you idiot." She jumped down next to me and inspected the wound. It was dripping only a small amount of blood. Most of the damage was probably internal.

"I'll be alright, the device will help patch me up good. Christian needs more help than me," I said.

She ran off toward the room with the fireplace picking up a dagger which had been dropped on the floor. A couple minutes later she returned with long strips of red leather and chunks of padding butchered from the seats. Then she began the process of patching everyone up. Christian's wound was so grave that two long red makeshift bandages had to be held in place across his chest.

"I'm afraid your efforts are in vain, young lady," he said.

"Not if you are as stubborn as I think you are," she awkwardly joked while tightening the last bandage. He laughed which, in turn, caused him to cough in pain.

Next to us the surviving knight was kneeling before his fallen companion and was praying. When finished he covered the dead knight's face with a cloth and drove his sword through his heart.

"We should relocate Christian to the fire in the other room." Dalton spoke for the first time.

With that, Dalton and the knight grabbed a hold of Christian and carried him off to the fireplace. I managed to pick myself up and follow suit. The bandage was doing an excellent job of retaining the blood inside me although I could not resist the urge to keep a hold of my side.

Christian was placed into what was left of one of the seats and I took up my place next to him.

"We're gonna make sure everyone upstairs is alright. Just stay here for a few minutes," Jess instructed as the others left the room leaving me alone with Christian.

"This is too much." I sighed as I reclined into the seat keeping a firm hold of my wound.

"It's never too much, not until you have died trying," Christian said, his voice weak and tired.

"I don't really fancy dying, and I'm sick of everyone else dying; and don't get me started on all the killing, it's not all it's cracked up to be. Is it really worth it? I mean what will I have at the end of all this when everyone I've known is gone?" I asked.

Christian through his pain gave me a stern look. "Young sir, I will explain to you how I have achieved a life free from regret," he said trying to prop himself up on the seat with little success.

"Your quest which you have set yourself on is a journey. You begin a journey with only one step, but you also complete the journey with one step. If you follow your first step with your final step you turn around and all you see is the door from which you came." He broke off in a fit of coughing. "What is most important, are all the steps in between. Each and every obstacle, mistake and hardship you overcome is an extra step. If you continue on then you will have your final step, turn around and see the distance you have come with all the things you have accomplished behind you, you will be proud of the journey you have completed. This is why I am pleased with my own journey. Be a man who looks back at an incredible journey," Christian advised.

I was fairly surprised to hear such insightful words from this man, although I suppose it takes someone to have lived a great life to come up with great words.

"You have lost a lot, Griffin," he continued. "We all have, but you can lose so much more if you stop." He let out a painful bout of coughing.

"You sure know how to build someone up, don't you?" I smiled through the discomfort of my wound although it was slowly diminishing in pain.

"It is not the first time I have had to say such things. There have been others like you who have fought beside me and felt the same. Just extra steps on the journey, my friend," he explained closing his eyes. "If you do not mind, I must rest now."

Nodding in agreement I sat quietly and watched the bright flames flicker in the fireplace. Behind me through the doors was a chaotic scene of death but in front was a calm distracting warmth keeping my attention.

Chapter 18

Fallout

About ten minutes had passed when Dalton eventually returned on his own.

"We've rallied everyone upstairs and… ohh!" Dalton stopped mid-sentence, his gaze firmly locked on Christian who was slumped with his eyes closed. Without even realising it, Christian had passed away by my side.

"He was happy with what he'd done with his life," I spoke whilst propping myself up from the seat. "In the end, that's all that really matters."

Dalton nodded in agreement.

As I was about to leave the room Dalton stopped me in my tracks.

"We must ensure that his body cannot be used by the Remnant, it would be a disgrace to all he has worked toward," he said.

I stared back at Christian lying peacefully on the couch and then turned to Dalton.

"Do you think you could do it this time please? I'm not scared or anything, I just… this one time I'd rather not, I've already lost one friend today."

"Yes of course, Mr Holster. You just wait in the next room, I won't be a second," Dalton agreed sympathetically.

In the main chamber I waited for Dalton to do what was necessary. There was bloodshed everywhere in the midst of which was Ophanim's lifeless corpse. I wandered over and just stared at it, bullet ridden with a large hole where Christian's blade had sliced clean through Ophanim's heart. Suffering a brief moment of anger I lashed out with my foot, kicking his corpse full force in the side.

"Fucking coward," I muttered under my breath.

"It's done," Dalton announced as he joined me and picked up the briefcase housing the drone which had been tossed to one side during all the commotion. One of the knights was standing guard at the spiral staircase and muttered a single word as we approached.

"Christian?"

I shook my head in dismay and the knight nodded in understanding. He was about to head for the room whilst removing his sword from the sheath before Dalton stopped him. He patted his own chest and nodded to indicate he had already done what was necessary and the knight nodded back and sheathed his sword.

We headed up the cold staircase till we reached the secret entrance. Jess was waiting for us looking flushed and out of breath.

"Something is going on in the town. Quickly, follow me," she huffed before turning around and scooting back outside. Following hurriedly we arrived to the walkway overlooking the town.

Scores of people were lining the streets all heading away from the castle, some of whom were hooded and leading regular dressed people away as prisoners.

"This does not look good," I said.

"We should give this situation a greater inspection," Dalton suggested opening up the briefcase.

The metallic ball was still flaking chunks of black tar when he placed it on the floor. A second later the ball swirled open causing a small layer of black residue to land underneath it. Free from its shell the drone switched on and hovered above the casing. All the screens illuminated into life showing an image of us staring at the flying mechanism.

"Alright, still operational, let us go and have a little ponder," Dalton whispered to himself whilst in full concentration at the controls of the drone.

Guiding the device across the sky toward the amassing crowds, Dalton and the rest of us were glued to the screens in anticipation. Floating high across the sky unnoticed the drone managed to gain a decent vantage point.

Hundreds of people were lining the streets, men, women and children all either screaming or wearing the hooded gowns of the cultists.

I had gotten vaguely used to seeing men and women being part of the possessed group but I had not yet witness a child being brought into their world. It was a new kind of wrong which I could not cope with seeing or thinking about.

Zooming in we could see two possessed holding up a staff each, one containing a prism above and the other the double circle symbol. Ahead of them was an extremely large building with a flat wall – perfect for the portal to be projected onto.

It seemed like the cultists had resorted to a final plan B of all out carnage, their usual attempts of hiding in secret and abducting people no longer possible. Large amounts of Remnant creatures poured out of the oversized portal onto the street where line after line of local people were kept ready for mass possession. Amongst the regulars were a couple of flying Remnant and even one of the tentacle scorpion-looking creatures which looked extremely confused at why it could not burrow through the concrete and had to resort to scuttling along the floor and vanishing between buildings.

"Oh God, what do we do?!" Jess exclaimed in shock and horror.

Then it came. Towering above all the other Remnant. First a leg, then the body, a necklace of skulls and then the horned head of Malphas entering our world.

"Hoooooly shhhhit!" I let out.

Without hesitation Dalton jumped up from the controls, positioned the rifle on a railing and took aim down the scope. Inhaling a large breath he waited a second then very slowly exhaled and let off one round of the rifle. Looking back to the drone screens the glass prism shattered into pieces, raining glass onto a group of confused possessed.

Destroying the prism instantly shut down the portal but it was too late as Malphas had already completely emerged.

The giant monstrosity turned to see his gateway collapsed, his face enraged and covered in newly formed cuts and gashes from the explosion. His chest expanded as he took in air and then he let out the loudest and most low pitched Remnant roar I'd heard. Swinging his arm in a complete frenzy he smashed into the wall where the portal had been, blow after blow dented the wall until a hole appeared.

Meanwhile the hundreds of people scattered in a panic, managing to break free in the uproar. Remnant started chasing after them in all directions. Malphas turned back to where the shot had come from and pointed directly toward us commanding his followers to retrieve us.

Hoards redirected their attention toward us, allowing people to flee from their grasp, although anyone who got in their way was now cut down without hesitation or remorse.

"I think we have a problem," I stated.

"What the hell do we do?" Jess questioned Dalton who himself looked a little distressed. He was stuck in thought, watching the masses approach whilst trying to concentrate.

"Well? What do we do?!" Jess repeated in a panic.

"I'm thinking, Goddamn it." Dalton sounded stressed, but everyone stared at him in hope.

"OK… The tunnel system entrance is nearby."

"But some of it is flooded, remember," I said.

"Yes, but we can at least lose them, then we find a safe place to exit and we can acquire a vehicle of some sort. I will contact the pilot to rendezvous with us in a secure location," he explained.

Flying Remnant were already circling close by so as a group we headed back inside and down to the main courtyard where the last of the knights gathered.

"Time to go!" I shouted over to them.

Stopping at the front entrance we gave everyone the chance to assemble closely.

"OK, as soon as this door opens, Mr Holster will sprint for the tunnel system and we follow," Dalton instructed. A few faces remained with blank expressions and he realised his mistake and repeated the instructions in Romanian. He then received more convincing looks of acknowledgment.

Sweat ran down the side of my head and I began bobbing up and down becoming nervous. I gripped the pistol with more strength than was physically necessary and my eyes focused on the doorway. The pain in my side was minimal now as all my concentration was diverted to this one task. Dalton pushed the door slightly with his hand then kicked it full force.

"GO, GO, GO!"

My legs reacted before I even knew what I was doing. I was out the door and heading toward the tunnel entrance. Seconds later all I could hear was gunfire and wings swooping down behind me. I continued running without turning back as the noise escalated. A man screamed but I did not turn back to look, I just kept running. One of the Remnant swooped down in front of me and I ducked while spraying rounds blindly into it whilst holding the top of my head with the free hand. Letting out a Remnant roar it flew away. For some reason my wrist device did not fire. I must have been in such a panic that I did not even think about firing but had done so on impulse.

Keeping my pace I was in the forest and almost by the entrance. A woman screamed behind me amid the chaos and the sudden thought of it being Jess made me turn to look. One of the knights was being flown off past the treetops in the firm grasp of the Remnant. To my selfish relief Jess was still behind me. My moment of weakness caused me to trip while not watching where I was going.

"Shit!" I uttered.

A Remnant dove down at me but one of the knights sliced its abdomen spraying blue blood across me. The beast sprawled on the ground hacking at anything and everything until the knight buried his sword in its chest. Dalton dragged me up from my feet and I continued.

Reaching the trap door I pushed the shrubbery to one side and heaved the wooden hatch up. Large vibrations began echoing up my legs, watching the group catch up to me I saw a huge darkness forming behind them through the trees. Trees could be heard collapsing in the distance and the shadow began forming a giant figure. My eyes widened in horror.

I jumped into the hole catching a hold of the ladder and hopping down to the bottom. Dalton and the others followed close behind as the floor shook even more violently. As the last knight attempted to jump down the shaft his legs had entered but an enormous claw sideswiped his body causing the lower half of the man to drop down next to the group as the rest of him disappeared from sight.

"LET'S GET MOVING PEOPLE!" I screamed. There was no time to take in the horrific fate of our ally. Jess was standing in shock staring at the torso-less body.

"MOVE, JESS!" I screamed. We sprinted down past the water streaming in as a roar boomed through the caverns with an intensity I had never heard before. I was forced to cover my ears to stop them imploding in my head.

The combination of the roar and vibrations caused the rest of the tunnel to collapse behind us, preventing any more Remnant following.

Only four of the knights remained from the original group including the couple who had saved me in the village. We jogged down the tunnel till we entered a split in our path, one way led to the village while the other led behind the castle and away from the madness.

Dalton started down the path away from the village and I followed right behind.

"Griff!" Jess shouted from behind. I turned to find Jess standing with the knights facing the other direction.

"There are still hundreds of people in the village," she protested. I turned to look back toward the tunnel leading away and then back at her.

"Miss Hart, you saw what was happening, there is nothing we can do–"

"Don't you Miss Hart me, Dalton, and don't you lecture me on what can and can't be done!" she raged, pointing her finger into his face.

"Jess… there is an army of them up there. We will probably die and if I die then the whole place goes up anyway." I tried to be sympathetic. Her expression turned less angry and more thoughtful as she looked at me.

"Griff, if we go, we still have to live knowing we just let people die. If we go back and we die, then it is without regret… Do you think Jasper and Bill would be happy knowing after all we've done we just ran away?"

I looked at her with the pain of remembering Bill and Jasper's demise.

"They died knowing we could save people. If we start sacrificing hundreds of people then where does it end? Next time it's thousands then millions," she reasoned.

She had a point. I could not bring myself to be a bad person; I could not allow myself to be the judge and executioner of all those people.

"It is for the good of mankind that we rid the world of those things," Dalton interrupted.

"What is the good of mankind, if mankind is not good, Dalton? Jess is right." I walked over to be by her side and watched Dalton decide what to do. He stroked his chin and licked his lips whilst moving his eyes around the room searching for an answer.

"Very well, we go back and give the people time to get away, but even so, we cannot save all of them. You know this to be correct."

"As long as we try, that is what matters," Jess told him.

I knew Dalton would agree to help us. It was only his unending sense of logical thinking which prevented him from sometimes doing what was right, but his sense of reason was still working fine and I had begun to believe this man had a good heart.

"I think I might have a plan as well," I mentioned. They both turned and looked at me in surprise.

"Yeah I know, it happens sometimes, that I get ideas," I joked. To be honest it was a bit of a lie – it was more of a general idea than a fully thought out plan.

"Well, what is it?" Jess questioned curiously.

"It's kind of a work in progress but, we will need a distraction to lure Malphas to us and we will also need a getaway vehicle as Dalton said before."

"So you wish to lure out one of the most powerful Remnant? It does not sound like much of a plan, Mr Holster, but I am intrigued" Dalton said.

Dalton then proceeded to translate to the Romanians.

"OK, well, the knights are pleased to have us and agree to escort any civilians out of danger while we do whatever you have in mind. Also might I add, Christian's house is rigged to explode to remove all evidence of the knights plans if compromised, or so I have been informed by our accomplices here," Dalton explained.

"Sounds good. We need to set off that explosion to distract the Remnant while the knights evacuate the people. Meanwhile we find a car to get us away," I said.

Everyone agreed.

"Right then, let's go!"

Chapter 19

Tunnel vision

How many times is it now that things have gotten out of hand or the world seems to want me dead? More importantly, how many times have I started to agree to dive into these perilous situations head first on my own accord? It is becoming a negative habit on my part. My mind was curious as to why Dalton agreed to change his mind so rapidly to escort us into the village. Perhaps he felt he owed us for rescuing him or maybe he was just too tired to argue anymore.

Travelling down the tunnel system we neared a set of ladders leading up to an exit. Muffled sounds came from above and as we continued to close in on the noise it became clear they were screams of villagers desperately attempting to escape.

Jess and I stood for a second staring up at the hatch.

"Nothing to be done from here," said Dalton walking past. Jess turned and followed the group as the remaining knights led the way. I stood for an extra second staring at the motionless hatch before regrouping as well.

The ground vibrated against my feet slightly. I assumed it was Malphas terrorising above us but as we journeyed further down the catacombs the vibrations greatly enhanced causing the support beams to scatter dirt and make worrying groaning sounds.

"Is he following us?" I asked Dalton confused.

"I don't know how he could be. We are fairly deep underground to be emitting any kind of heat signature for him to track," he replied.

Walking further the ground shook once more.

"Something's not right," I said.

As we paced further the left wall began to shake violently and gave off a loud rumbling noise. Dirt dropped in clumps onto the floor and a small hole emerged and grew rapidly in size.

"Erm… I think we'd better go a little faster," I suggested.

Something blue wriggled inside the growing hole in the wall. Everyone moved past hugging the opposite wall. A long shelled tentacle slithered out of the wall feeling along the floor while occasionally flashing in and out of reality. Finger-sized spikes were on the underside of the tentacle leaving scratch marks in the mud.

Being the last member of the group to edge around the tentacle I raised my device aiming it in the hole in the wall. Fire.

Crack, whistle.

Shell began distorting, crumpling in on itself and sounding like a sheet of paper being rustled up into a ball. This was followed by a high pitched gargle as if the creature had a mouth full of liquid. The rest of the tentacle detached from the creature and wriggled freely on the floor. Some blue blood stained the hole but otherwise it was dark with no other movement or sound.

"Well, that was pretty easy," I said joining the rest of the group.

Walking a couple of yards down the path the vibrations through the floor started again. Stopping, I turned to look over my shoulder and, a second later, the wall burst into a thousand small pieces firing in all directions. My face was covered from the debris but I managed to spot more tentacles through the cloud of dirt and dust. My eyes widened in horror as the beast slowly emerged from the fallout. It had six beady blue red eyes hiding under the front of its shell with a large beak at the very front. Gunfire sounded as the group fired a stream of bullets at the creature causing it to recoil slightly and place its shelled tentacles in front of its body to protect itself from the oncoming fire.

Without any second thoughts I turned back around and took off down the blackened tunnel.

"Run, run, run, run, run!" I yelled running past the group. I think they kind of got the idea but I could not stop myself saying it.

Panting erratically I stopped at a junction in the catacombs. I had gotten a little ahead of the group under the influence of the device charge. Watching the rest catch up through the flickering of torchlights I saw the monster crashing through the tunnels behind them. The ground shook as section after section of tunnel collapsed behind the beast's trail of destruction.

"We'll never outrun that thing, we have to split up and try to get behind it," I suggested as everyone caught up.

There was no time to rethink. Jess, two knights and I ran right as Dalton and the other two knights ran left. Entering a large opening I looked back down the darkened passage to find the creature was nowhere in sight. Waiting a couple of seconds the rumbling of the floor decreased in magnitude and I deduced it must have followed after the other group.

"OK, let's go back," I ordered, forgetting the knights could not understand me. I just pointed back and they nodded in agreement.

Again we ran down the pitch black tunnel except this time toward the rumbling path of the creature. Appalling beastly noises were coming from up ahead with the presence of gunfire and the flashing of light beams from the torches coming from another large cavern. I quickly glanced at the wrist device and saw the blue lights had worn off. Up ahead I could see the outline of the oversized scorpion monster flash between light beams and gunshot flashes.

They were stuck in a stalemate as the group could not fire past the beast's tentacles and the monster could not attack as it would leave itself vulnerable. I didn't dare get too close in case it flipped around and gave me a good hiding. Staying the maximum distance the wrist device could reach I took aim at the monster, only then realising, I had no idea where its heart actually was…

I decided the best option was to take aim directly down the centre, right at the top of its shell to uncover what was underneath. The crosshairs skimmed the top of the shell. Fire.

Crack, Whistle.

Blue shell cracked in on itself revealing a heap of purplish organs throbbing inside the body. The shot also managed to rip through two of the front tentacles covering its face. It went into a complete frenzy, the shot had gone through its eyes, causing it to swing violently not knowing where anything was.

"Where the fuck is its heart?!" I shouted over to Dalton on the opposite side of the flailing creature.

"I don't know! Just shoot the damn thing!" he shouted back trying to avoid its swinging tentacles.

Phasing in and out of time made the creature even harder to avoid as a tentacle could be flying one direction then suddenly disappear and return heading right for me. People were shooting at the creature from all directions and it cried out with its watery groan as bullets ricochet from the shell with a couple penetrating the gaping hole in its back. Eventually it slowed down and collapsed in a heap in the centre of the cavern.

Jess walked a little closer to the motionless monster.

"Woah there, Jackie!" I snatched her back by the arm.

"What are you doing?" she questioned in annoyance.

"If it was dead it would have disappeared by now. It's trying to trick us, the sneaky little bugger," I explained.

She stood and inspected the creature from a distance.

"It looks pretty dead to me," she said.

Dalton was on the opposite side of the beast raising his head and attempting to peek inside the huge gap in the exoskeleton. He raised his rifle and sprayed a few rounds into it. The creature suddenly burst back into life, scuttling about giving off one last groan before once again falling under its own weight whilst twitching a few times. It dispersed out of existence in a flurry of red mist.

To be completely honest, it had gone better than expected. Just the good old fashioned shoot it till it's dead approach, although without the wrist device I imagine it would be a lot more difficult to get inside it's shell. I was proud that I'd learned from past experience to know it was not properly dead, but I just hoped there were no more of those things hanging about.

"Excellent, how about we hop along now?" Dalton asked over the silence as we all just stared at the blue stain on the floor.

"They just don't stop do they?" Jess huffed.

"True story," I responded before following her back down the tunnel. On the bright side, the tremors had subsided and with the beast now gone, it didn't feel like I was going to be buried alive after all which is always a bonus.

Marching behind the knights we arrived at an unfamiliar set of ladders. The underground way to Christian's house had gradually become more and more flooded and was now inaccessible leaving us with only one option – to take the closest exit and sneak as quietly as possible through the village above.

One of the knights went up first, pushing the hatch over to one side, it remained dark. We followed closely behind. It was cramped in the small room and the floor clanged as I walked on the metallic surface. At one end one of the knights cautiously pushed a bar to open half of the wall with minimum sound. Light flooded in casting the knight's shadow on the opposite wall. After peering out he nodded to us and pushed the door far enough to squeeze through. I wandered out into the fresh cool air of the night once more.

Chapter 20

Disaster Zone

Artificial floodlight was cast across a large fenced-off yard filled with old buses, trucks and large metal containers. Only a few buildings surrounded the complex located next to a main road. There was no imminent sign of threat or for any person at all in the vicinity. It was fairly quiet nearby although in the distance there were muffled Remnant roars with the shadow of a flying Remnant gliding over the moonlit sky far away.

"OK, so, first we need to get to Christian's house and find out how to blow it up. Looks like we have our getaway vehicles, if we can get any of them to work. They will be good to get the villagers out but we probably still need something a little faster," I suggested.

"Seems to be the plan," Dalton concurred.

"Out of the frying pan…. And into the village filled with bloodthirsty demonic creatures," I joked before setting off toward the yard entrance.

A small brick building was inside the yard and my best guess was that any keys for the vehicles were stored inside. I arrived at the door and attempted to kick the door down and, failing miserably, felt slightly ashamed as one of the knights wandered over and provided enough force behind his boot to smash the wooden door from the lock.

"Thanks," I said shamefully.

Scouting the office area I sifted through some filing cabinets and drawers. As one of the desk drawers was locked I decided to use my master key. Pointing my device straight downwards I fired.

Wood cracked in on itself as did the concrete floor below it. A long hole formed in the ground but the drawer now also had a gaping hole in it so all was good. I gave it a second for the beam to finish destroying the desk and floor before inspecting the drawer. All the keys were inside and labelled up with number plate references. Sadly a few of the keys may have been caught in the gravitational field and were missing chunks.

"Oops!"

I grabbed them all anyway and ran back into the yard. Dalton was looking over one of the old buses. Checking the number plate and comparing it to the note on the keys I found that particular vehicle's key to be unusable.

"Maybe we should try a different bus?" I asked Dalton who was hanging from the door looking inside.

"There does not seem to be anything problematic about this vehicle," he explained.

"Erm, I think there is," I said holding out the damaged key.

"How did you manage that?" Jess asked stunned.

"Well I didn't mean to do it, did I? I had to shoot the lock off the drawer and it kind of took half the keys with it," I replied.

"Griff, you can be a right idiot sometimes. What keys are still alright then?" she enquired harshly.

Frowning I held out my hands and scoured the remaining keys.

"These three." I held up the keys whilst discarding the rest on the floor. Jess and Dalton both had a quick gaze around for the corresponding number plates.

"So we have… One waste disposal vehicle and two buses. Let us hope they are still somewhat operational," Dalton said.

"Well that's OK, isn't it? Fill the two buses full of people and use the rubbish truck to bash anything blocking the street," I suggested.

"If they are even functional then, yes," Dalton replied.

One of the knights climbed into the rubbish truck and managed to turn on the engine. He smiled and gave the universal thumbs up.

"Well at least we have that one," Jess acknowledged.

Dalton once again had a quick chat with the knights in their native language, one of whom handed him a key.

"We can get into Christian's house with this key. The manual trigger for the explosives is in his preparation room behind the map of the area and I've been informed it is relatively straight forward to activate. These fine people have agreed to wait for the distraction then collect as many survivors as possible. In the meantime whilst one of us set off the device the other two of us can search for a vehicle, if we have not already located a sufficient one on the path toward the house," Dalton said.

"Sounds good," I concurred.

Dalton took out his phone which was surprisingly still in one piece and proceeded to ring someone.

"Ready evac, may arrive at the rendezvous under hostile conditions," he instructed before terminating the call.

Gunshots cracked off in the distance followed by yelling Remnant and faint screams of people – it was grim to hear.

"Well… No point just waiting around to die," Jess said inspecting the entrance to the compound. It had been left ajar as if someone had left in a hurry, which was not surprising given the circumstances. She pushed the gate open and wandered out into the empty street.

Dalton and I followed her. The knights stayed behind and one of them was kind enough to wave us off. Sticking to the edges of the road we began our journey into the village toward Christian's house. As we drew closer the sounds of Remnant and people alike became louder. One of the wooden houses was ablaze in the night as the rest of the street seemed abandoned. Another particular house had the front door smashed in with claw marks across the walls. I grimaced as I imagined the horror the occupants must have felt.

Humming of an engine approached and we took cover behind one of the old cars parked on a driveway. Round the corner came an old banged up car containing an entire family. The man driving seemed to have his eyes completely wide and focused on the road and looked an extremely pale shade of ghostly white as they escaped the town.

"Can we take this car?" I asked leaning against the light brown chassis.

"Well it is a possibility, but I sincerely believe we could accommodate something a little more effective for the situation," Dalton explained.

"So that's a no then, that's all you had to say… No," I replied sternly, becoming annoyed by his elongated speeches.

"There's no need for bickering, let's just get to the house and find something better," Jess interrupted.

Carrying on carefully through the streets a shadow passing between buildings on the opposite side of the road caught my eye followed by the sound of wood crunching to pieces. I carried on with anxiety. A flying Remnant was circling in the sky not so far away but seemed more preoccupied with something else as it swooped down to a different street.

"They're just everywhere, it's crazy," I whispered.

Watching my footing I hopped between gardens. Our torches were off for obvious reasons and the only sources of light were the purplish moon and the burning building.

"Are we even going the right way?" I asked quietly.

"We certainly are. Andrei pointed me in the correct direction," Dalton replied.

"Who the hell is Andrei?" I enquired.

"One of the remaining knights. It helps to learn the names of new acquaintances, Mr Holster."

Loud yelling came from one of the opposite houses whilst a dog barked madly. We stopped and took cover behind a fence. Peering through the gap between the planks I saw a light in the top window of an old wooden house. Within seconds there was another loud yell of a man before his body smashed through the window causing glass to shatter. The well-built curly blond-haired man just lay half out the window with one arm hanging limp. Light from the room was soon blocked out by the hulking shadow of a Remnant before the body was dragged back through the window. A golden retriever ran out of the smashed up front door and continued to sprint away down the street.

"It's too late for him," Dalton whispered as we carried on.

"At least the dog got away," I whispered to Jess.

Arriving on the main street we gathered behind a large restaurant building. This seemed to be where the bulk of the Remnant force were. Even as they had dissipated across the area there was still a large convergence of Remnant roaming this specific street. I could see Bran Castle from here, or at least what was left of it. Malphas was demolishing the building top to bottom with his overpowering strength, like some kind of living wrecking ball.

"Destruction of such a historical masterpiece is a sin in itself. Perhaps we should make haste," Dalton urged.

I couldn't have agreed more.

Choice of transportation was scarce as most working vehicles had already been taken by people attempting to flee the area. Most of the remaining ones had been badly damaged by the Remnant.

Managing to slowly gain ground by sneaking around the back of the buildings, I spotted Christian's house just a little further down on the other side of the street. There were Remnant patrolling the streets and disappearing in and out of buildings.

"Right, if I go in the house and set off the bomb will you two have a car ready for me outside to get away?" I asked.

"We can try our best. Just make sure you get out in time," Jess replied.

"Don't worry I'll run like the clappers."

Jess smiled at me making light of the situation. "Just get out, OK? We'll see you in a bit."

Good luck, Mr Holster." Dalton patted my shoulder and placed the door key in my hand before the pair of them left in the opposite direction leaving me on my own.

Sliding the key into my jacket pocket I crouched against the building and popped my head around the corner facing the empty street. It was unnerving watching random Remnant creatures dashing between buildings. My foot twitched up and down in anticipation. I waited till there were no enemies in sight before sprinting straight across the street. Without looking back I reached the opposite side and dived over some bushes in the front garden of some house.

Peeking up I was relived to find no wave of monsters heading in my direction. I circled around the back of the building and proceeded down to Christian's house whilst ducking behind any object on my way just in case something happened to stumble in my direction.

A loud crashing sound echoed from the building next to Christian's just as I arrived. I kept my eyes fixated on the back door while edging to where I needed to be. With my back firmly gripped to the wall I slid around to the front of the house. It seemed to me in all my optimism like our efforts were futile as I could not imagine anyone surviving an invasion of these monsters – it took only a handful to annex an island.

To my dismay the front door was already slightly ajar, surely the place should have blown up if someone had broken in?

"Are you in, Griff?" Jess's voice came from my collar causing me to jump out of my skin. I had completely forgotten about the small communication device. I held in the button on the small rectangular object to speak.

"Jesus, you almost killed me. I'm not in yet but it looks like someone was already here, I'll call you when I'm done," I whispered in reply.

"Alright, sorry, be careful in there," Jess said. I shook my head in disbelief at the unnecessary shock I had received and then pressed the mute button.

My wrist device arrow was pointing into the building behind me which was reassuring although I could not let my guard down so easily. Removing my pistol from my side I turned on the light and squeezed through the gap in the door trying not to disturb it or cause any avoidable sound.

The place was a tip and it was clear the place had been ransacked. Claw marks tore through the walls as I passed my light over the hallway. Flowers and tiny pieces of the vase were scattered across the floor with the table in two halves collapsed on the floor. Stepping over the mess I carefully made my way up the wooden stairs, holding my breath with every footstep and trying to tiptoe as quietly as possible.

I crept to the end room upstairs. The door was hanging from the bottom hinges at an angle, the concept of using a door handle must be too much for the Remnant to comprehend. Pushing the damaged door to one side I entered to find a body lying in the centre of the room, which I recognised to be one of the knights or at least what was left of him.

"Damn," I said, feeling slightly nauseated.

Blood stained the man's clothes and the floor. He had a huge hole gaping from his back where his heart would have been. This explains why the alarms never went off at least, he must have escaped the Remnant, but then, how? And why would he have a hole in his chest? Was he possessed? The Remnant wouldn't kill their own? So many thoughts ran through my mind but it didn't matter, I stepped over the corpse finding the map luckily untouched, so I ripped it from the wall revealing a large hole containing a collection of wires and circuit boards hooked up to a very basic eight bit display. There were a couple of switches and buttons all marked up. Surprisingly auto and manual as well as a start button were all in English, or perhaps the Romanian is the same as English? It didn't matter now.

As I was inspecting the circuitry and needlessly pondering the language of the writing I felt a sudden change in the atmosphere of the room. It was one of those horrible sixth sense feelings that I was being watched. I stopped still and looked down by my side. Huge black and red scaly claws were slowly passing between my waist and arm. My eyes widened and I stared at the claw, it was just like in my nightmares from my time in the hospital. In sheer panic and fear I went to twist around as fast as I could but my right arm was instantly grabbed and pulled to one side rendering my device and pistol useless. This must be it.

Chapter 21

The Returned

The power behind the grasp of my arm was incredible. The scaly black claw pulled my arm around with such force that I twisted on the spot a full 180 degrees. When my body came to a standstill my other arm was grabbed so that there was no escape or any chance of retaliation. Standing in front of me was a towering Remnant staring into my eyes. Although stuck in sheer terror, something seemed different, its red and blue eyes didn't look entirely menacing and it held its mouth closed instead of showing its crazed grin. I squinted my eyes in confusion at why I was still alive. Then, to my complete surprise in its raspy low voice it uttered one word.

"Griffin…"

Now at this point my brain was going into overdrive. This Remnant had just said my name, or had I mistaken my name for a low grumbling noise? I also realised with the long passage of time that not once had the Remnant phased out of reality like usual, and what was even more unusual was the fact that I was still alive.

"Hello…?" I asked without blinking or breaking eye contact for a second.

Before I received an answer or was inflicted with death a tall middle aged man holding a baseball bat walked through the door, I didn't recognise him as one of the knights and he didn't seem at all worried about the giant beast in front of me which led me to the conclusion that he was probably possessed. He looked at me and with a smirk uttered some strange words to the Remnant.

Seconds passed and nothing happened. The man began to seem confused at why nothing was happening, him and me both. He walked closer and shouted something at the large demonic creature. It turned its head away from me to look at the man.

"I think it's broken," I joked although I knew that now was probably not the time for humour.

Becoming completely enraged the man went to swing the bat at me and I flinched and twisted my face away. There was no pain. I'm pretty sure being hit in the face with a bat is meant to be painful. The Remnant had let go of my wrists and had a firm hold of the wooden bat. Clenching its claw shut caused the bat to splinter into pieces before the top half fell to the floor with a clunk.

Bemused by what had occurred the man stared at the remains of the bat handle and then at the beast. Before he could even question what had happened the Remnant grabbed his face engulfing it in its claw. He let off a muffled screamed into the scaly skin of the beast as he was lifted off his feet. The monster lunged forward and forced the man's head into the wall causing it to concave and erupt a flood of darkened blood onto the surroundings.

"Oh, fuck!" I let out as the body crumpled to the floor decapitated, blood and brain matter spraying up the wall in all directions.

Instantly I raised my newly freed arm pointing my device at the monster. It turned to face me with blood still dripping from its arm and side.

"Why?!" I shouted at it. Bringing one of its fingers up to its chest it pointed at itself.

"It's… Bill…" It spoke in a raspy tone.

Well, if only you could even imagine the look on my face right now, sheer dumbfounded with a small dose of bewilderment. Time went by with me just staring idiotically at this monster, blood still slowly sliding from the tip of its claws. I think my brain had just lost it as I let out a short, loud, laugh.

"Ha ha ha… Explain how please?" I humoured the beast keeping the orange target trained on its chest.

"Pulled. Through. Portal… Take. Remnant. Heart… Back. Through. Portal…" it explained in short bursts pointing at its heart. "Killed. Remnant. Mind…" it said pointing to its head.

It would explain why it had not yet phased away like the rest of them. The possibility of being able to possess them back in their plane of existence never crossed my mind. Being so, the chances of this monster being Bill were so incredible it was just unbelievable! Yet the facts provided made sense, most of all I wasn't dead and being not dead is working well in its favour. Even if I entertained the prospect of this being Bill, I didn't know a great deal about him to be able to ask personal questions. This was the first time I'd heard a Remnant speak properly as well as not attempt to kill me. I highly doubt as Bill was burning alive he would have explained who he was to the monster so I couldn't take the chance of it not being him. Besides, Bill or not, this thing would come in very handy helping me get away.

He was still waiting for me to say something. It was so strange having this monster who is possibly my friend being calm and not the vicious killing machine I'd become accustomed to.

"Alright then, let's just say for a second you are Bill and I believe you, do you feel any different, like the need to kill everything around you?" I questioned.

"Not. For. You…" Bill answered.

"I don't really know how reassuring that is, Bill, but it's better than nothing," I said.

It was strange calling this creature Bill. It would be so easy just to kill it and not have to worry about it further.

"Well, I'm going to blow up this whole building, Bill, then Jess and Dalton are going to pick us up and we are getting the hell out of here," I explained turning back around to the circuitry.

"Ophanim…?" Bill asked.

"He was a bad guy. I mean he's now a dead bad guy so no worries there. He shut the portal behind you and also murdered and tortured a lot of innocent people so no love lost," I told him.

"Told…You…" Bill replied.

"Yeah you certainly did." I was figuring out if it was literally just a simple case of pressing start or if I had to set a time and I realised then that only the real Bill could have known about the conversation we had about his doubts on Ophanim, it must really be him.

Flicking the switch from auto to manual I pressed the start button. I couldn't help thinking to myself that something so dangerous should probably have some kind of password or other safety device on, but then again I'm in Romania, who am I to judge their safety standards? The timer kicked into life with a mere two minutes to escape.

"Time to go." I turned around to see Bill already crouching under the doorframe to exit. I followed him through and down the hallway, his black and red reptile-like back bobbing up and down as he went with his claw like hands just hovering above the floor instead of dragging along like the Remnant usually do. Subtle little differences like this in his mannerisms helped me believe he really was Bill.

Bill was half way down the stairs when I reached the top and heard a horrible screeching roar from the bottom. Another Remnant creature hurled itself up at Bill, tackling him through the bannisters and down to the floor. We really didn't have time for this. I jumped half way down the stairs and aimed my wrist device but it became the classic case of who was who. Watching as the two of them were scrapping it out I kept my arm trained on them until eventually one of them phased in and out of reality. Quickly I aimed and shot at the monster with the device.

It let off another screech as its left arm was torn and detached from its body. The shot continued through to the wall creating a hole to the next room and into the ground. Bill took this opportunity to pick up the monster by its head and torso with his newly found strength. It swung wildly with its remaining arm until it was thrown onto the sharp broken bannister impaling it multiple times. Trapped but not dead it wriggled trying to break free. I risked getting close and fired multiple times into its chest with my pistol.

There was no time to lose. I couldn't afford to make sure it was completely dead, in a few seconds it wouldn't matter anyway. I had to get as far away as possible from the building.

"Get a move on!" I shouted down at Bill as I jumped the rest of the stairs to the bottom.

Sprinting out the door with the influence of the device's electrical charge I managed to keep pace with Bill. There were a couple of Remnant to our right a few buildings down who didn't hesitate to give chase. We dodged to the left and ran like hell, the anticipation of the explosion was killing me. I didn't even know how large of an explosion it would be.

Only reaching about three buildings down the road I looked back and it happened. Starting at the base of the building a small fire erupted out of the windows. As the Remnant ran past the whole bottom floor blew in all directions hurling debris at the monsters which were engulfed in a fireball. The force of the blast even threw one of the Remnant up against the building on the opposite side of the street. The top floor then also blew in all directions throwing a mass of bricks and wood everywhere. I was thrown off my feet and I smashed into the ground scraping my face along the pavement. There was no sign of the Remnant following us and the buildings neighbouring Christian's house were almost all gone and set in flames. A huge thick smoke cloud bellowed up into the night sky lit up by the flames below.

Chapter 22

Death Race

Sore from the graze on the side of my face I brushed a small quantity of tiny stones from my cheek. I coughed as a mist of dust spread through the street from the explosion. Pushing up with both arms I was assisted by one of Bill's huge claws to reach a standing position.

"Thanks," I coughed.

Upright and staring through the flames I saw the outline of what remained of Bran Castle; a once glorious structure reduced to rubble. A huge black shadow of Malphas dropped from the ruins. There was no way to see any facial expressions from such a distance but I could tell we had caught his attention.

Thunderous in volume the otherworldly creature roared into the night, undoubtedly being heard all across the area.

"He's. Not. Happy…" Bill groaned.

"No, he certainly is not," I agreed.

He began a charge toward us from the castle grounds. At the same time a car horn sounded from the opposite direction. Looking back to see what was coming I saw a disappointingly tiny looking vehicle with a Dacia badge on the front which looked like it should have belonged in a museum not on the road.

A gunshot rang out and Bill was struck in his hip. The initial strike caused him to flinch but otherwise he remained fine, if not looking a little angrier.

"Woah woah woah!" I shouted putting myself between Bill and the line of fire. Jess and Dalton were in the car looking at me as if I was insane, which if I'm being realistic is exactly what I would have thought if the roles were reversed.

"Don't shoot!" I screamed.

Dalton was driving as Jess was hanging out the window armed with the rifle. Tyres screeched as the car slid sideways to a halt next to us.

"What the hell is this?" I asked pointing out the joke of a car with both arms extended.

"I was going to ask you the same! What the fuck is wrong with you?!" Jess shouted keeping the rifle trained at Bill behind me.

The floor started to rumble, burning sections of the building behind were dropping off from the vibrations. Malphas was hurtling toward us from the very end of the road.

"Fuck this, get in the car," I ordered Bill as I opened the door.

"Are you mad, Griff it's a fucking monster!" she yelled again as I climbed into the small vehicle.

"Shit!" Jess screamed aiming her rifle right at Bill.

"Will you calm down? It's Bill alright!" I yelled back at her whilst slapping the rifle downwards out of her hands as Bill attempted to follow me into the car. His knees were basically in the front and his head arched over his shoulder right next to mine.

Dalton had no hesitation as he started to turn the car around.

"What do you mean Bill? Bill's dead!"

"Jess. Hart…" Bill said with what I could only imagine was an attempt at some sincerity in his growling voice.

"Bill…?" Jess replied in a softer voice.

"Aw, Bill, your breath reeks," I said as he exhaled onto my face as he spoke. Now I'm not proud at such a comment but if you could have smelt what I just did I believe some people would have said a lot worse. My guess is he didn't appreciate my comment as he gave me a look similar to that of a Remnant who wanted to kill me.

"As fascinating and as touching as your little reunion is, the issue still remains that we are currently being pursued by what can only be described as a demonic God." Dalton decided to join in the conversation.

Watching out the rear window there was Malphas closing in from a distance. Every so often he would disappear and then reappear a little closer.

"I possibly should mention that our LZ is in the opposite direction to which we are travelling," Dalton explained. This time I looked at him as if he was the idiot.

"Well then, get on the phone and tell your pilot pal to fly to the other side!" I shouted.

There was a strange whistling noise coming from behind while I wasn't watching, then raining from the sky was a full car which dropped only feet away from us, crunching into the road and almost flipping down onto us had Dalton not swerved just in time.

Dalton pulled the phone from his pocket whilst just remaining on the road with one hand on the wheel.

"Revision of LZ is required, relocate on phone GPS, swing round, area is highly compromised," he requested down the phone before replacing it into his pocket.

"Watch out!" Jess screamed pointing forward at a Remnant running out from the side of the road. It dived out at the car only just managing to claw at my door, three black talons ripping through only just missing my leg as all I could do was watch wide eyed. It could not hold on to the moving vehicle and soon tumbled backwards. I watched as it rolled in front of Malphas and was quickly thrown out of the way by the charging beast.

Jess fired two shots at the gigantic creature but it failed to even flinch. It just grinned in that horrific demonic manner.

"Bullets won't stop him, Dalton!" Jess shouted into the car.

He was still chasing and closing in fast, having originally lost a little pace when throwing the vehicle at us. The oversized monster phased away and on returning to reality had another small vehicle in his grasp.

"Watch out, Dalton, he's got another car!" I yelled forward.

Whistling noises grew closer again until the car dropped directly in front of us with a crunch of metal, plastic and rubber. Dalton swerved again but the back end of our car was clipped by the thrown car as it fell sideways causing us to skid to one side.

Now staring out the side window I was looking directly back down the street at Malphas. Clouds of condensed air blew from his nostrils as he breathed out, his scarred chest pumping in and out.

Squealing echoed from the engine once more as Dalton switched into first gear, I could smell smoke coming from the struggling motor as it gave everything it had to get us on the move.

Instead of turning back down the road Dalton stayed on course, smashing through a garden fence and squeezing between two buildings. As he managed to divert into the back garden the building erupted into a hail of wood and brick when Malphas burst through as if it weren't even an obstacle. The roof of the car began to dent and buckle as the remains of the building clattered down like heavy hail.

We rammed through the back fence just as easily as the front and almost collided with a tree. Dalton manoeuvred past and we found ourselves in the forest dodging more trees coming at us at all angles.

Terrain was ridiculously rough. Although Dalton was doing an excellent job being our designated rally driver it came at the cost of smashing my head on the car door and roof numerous times. The only reason Bill was not smashing off anything was that he was so cramped in the first place he could not move.

Becoming sick of rattling my brain I decided to open the car window via the manual handle, rolling it down gave me some much needed room by poking my head out the car.

Behind us Malphas was in the back garden hulking down through the dust and debris of the building he had just destroyed trying to spot where we had gone. We hadn't gotten far away and it didn't take long for him to charge after us again.

Matters were made worse by a small hoard of normal Remnant who had decided to join the chase. They were dashing through the trees as shadows disappearing and reappearing through the night. Our little Dacia was already struggling to keep up the pace against Malphas and was faring a lot worse with the added mixture of slippery mud, grass and rocks under the wheels.

Luckily the trees were just tightly packed enough to cause Malphas a small inconvenience, although his method of overcoming this problem was simply to bash through the forest like a bulldozer.

"How much ammo is left in the rifle Jess?" I shouted.

"Whatever's left in this clip!" she shouted back.

"I don't think it's gonna be enough!" I watched the mass of shadows follow us from all sides of the forest with the occasional flash of a limb when crossing the path of the torchlights.

They began closing in forcing Jess to fire. One of the Remnant was only a couple of feet away from the car as Jess shot into its face and chest causing it to screech and recoil. Another one approached my side of the car and leapt through the air as I aimed my device, the orange crosshairs lining up with its face I fired.

Crack, Whistle.

Its head was sucked into the twirling void. It attempted to let out some kind of scream but had no time as its body crashed into the side of the car and rolled backwards. The car swerved slightly but remained on course whilst Malphas behind had no hesitation in stomping on the wounded Remnant getting in the way.

Another Remnant latched itself to Jess's side of the car. It seemed extremely surprised to see another beast like itself sitting companion to us. In its second of hesitation Jess unloaded what remained of the rifle ammunition into the Remnant's back causing it to howl in anger and pain. Bill smashed through the side window and grabbed the beast's head with both hands tearing its jaw off. Overwhelmed and spraying blue blood onto the car the beast dropped off the vehicle tumbling along the ground.

"I'm out!" shouted Jess crouching back into the car.

Somehow through the illumination of the headlights we found ourselves on a dirt road where the Dacia could find a little more traction and gain a little more speed. Travelling in a more uphill direction the sound of helicopter blades whizzed through the air above and, to my delight, the faint outline of the copter was visible through the canopy.

Rupturing out the treeline from our rear, Malphas destroyed part of the forest throwing splinters of wood into the air. Above us the reassurance of seeing the getaway vehicle was undone by the presence of winged shadows circling the craft. Popping sounds echoed through the sky accompanied by extremely bright flares exploding in all directions from above. The helicopter had used its countermeasures and in doing so sent the flying Remnant into disarray without a reasonable thermal signature to chase after.

Floating down into the forest the flares brightened the area revealing a frightening amount of Remnant blitzing between the trees.

I watched as Malphas stopped his pursuit to launch a fully grown tree high up toward the origin of the bright flash of flares. Wincing through the extreme brightness I managed to witness the log narrowly avoid collision with the aerial vehicle but, in reaction to this, it banked sharply to the left and flew off on a different course.

Through the headlights I spotted a clearance in the trees. Dalton continued on, driving off the dirt road and onto the smooth grip of a proper road, he swerved and followed the road further up the mountain.

Climbing the steep road in our little Dacia we rose above the treetops and off in the distance I could now see what remained of Bran Castle. The surrounding village was smouldering in flames and was half destroyed. Was this far enough away to activate the capsule device?

Destruct.

Nothing happened, I looked at my wrist device and remembered the blue star shaped symbol which had to be completely folded over to activate the self-destruct. Only two corners of the star remained to fold into the centre, as we continued uphill another corner folded leaving just one.

Malphas charged onto the road, he took a second to see where we had vanished to and then gave chase, his face in complete rage.

The final section of the star folded to make a perfect circle and shot from the wrist device in the direction of Bran in a flash. Then a second later behind Malphas was the spectacle of green lights bursting from the ground around Bran Castle.

Chapter 23

Game Changer

Swirling around in a circle, the glowing lights formed a rotating dome around Bran. Buildings began to crumble into chunks of flying mass around the epicentre of the dome where the castle once stood. The castle itself had eviscerated within seconds, crunching in on itself.

Almost like a wave I could see row after row of trees lean toward the gravitational storm, the first few rows uprooting instantly and joining the ever growing bulk of rock. The ground shook violently as the earth was ripped apart and the gravitation pull reached the car.

Malphas was quite a way behind us and was struggling to keep himself in place, his enormous claws digging deep into the ground. Meanwhile the Dacia had come to a standstill yet I could hear the squealing of rubber against road. My body was firmly stuck against the back seat.

"Get us out of here, Dalton!" I shouted over the ever growing noise of the swirling rock storm tearing the ground apart.

"I'm applying maximum acceleration, Mr Holster! There's nothing more I can do!" he shouted back.

Worryingly the vehicle was very slowly beginning to be sucked backwards toward the storm and toward Malphas who was rooted to the spot. Smoke was bellowing from the wheels as we inched closer and closer. Malphas was digging in, his claws ripping chunks of the road out as he was pulled backwards.

Lights had turned from a green to an orange then a red flashing lightning around the massive rocky sphere spiralling in the air around a massive crater in the ground. I looked around to see some of the smaller

Remnant clutching onto trees and rocks, flying Remnant had perched themselves on top of mountains casually watching the destruction unfold from a safer distance.

Only a few feet away from Malphas even he showed signs of struggling, as he phased in and out of reality. Regardless of his efforts he began being dragged back down the road.

It felt like an earthquake had mixed together with a hurricane as high winds blew past battering the front window of the car with small rocks and branches while the ground shook violently. One specifically large branch hurtled into the glass at such a speed it left a large spider web like crack across the screen. Jess had her hands in front of her face expecting the eventual shattering of the window.

Unable to hold on any longer to the crumbling road, Malphas slid back at a large velocity into the treeline taking out multiple tree trunks on his way until he disappeared into the dark woods. Some of the smaller Remnant followed a similar fate whereas the rest managed to hold on for dear life.

It was a small relief that the large Remnant leader had vanished yet it did not make the situation any less dangerous as we could soon be heading for the same fate. As the swirling vortex of rock was emitting red bursts of light the rear of the car skidded along the road toward the edge of the forest.

Floating above the huge crater where Bran village once stood was the humongous moonlike sphere sucking up the surrounding area. Forest, vehicles, buildings and rock rotated around the sphere until in the blink of an eye the lights stopped and the floor stopped rumbling. In that instant the car jerked forward with the loss of drag and everything went dead quiet apart from the car we were in.

BOOOOOM!

A huge shockwave travelled across the sky as the massive floating orb erupted into millions of tiny particles scattering across the sky. The car was sent skidding sideways up the road and I held onto the seat with all my strength. Red lightning covered the night sky. Between the strokes of colour like a giant mirage I saw Helvius covered in Angious space craft and brightly coloured explosions from the ongoing power struggle for the planets portal devices – just like last time there was the monumental mushroom shaped metropolis dome city of the Angious, except this time it was perched on Helvius.

Before I could take in anymore the mirage disappeared and the car slammed into the side of a tree coming to an abrupt halt. I found myself breathing heavily and still clutching the seat even as everything calmed down. I looked next to me at Bill's new monstrous form and even he seemed relieved.

"Thank God," Jess uttered.

A perfectly round crater was all that was left of Bran. The surrounding area was stripped of forest and any notable landmarks and left completely barren. Through the perfect calm I just took in the scene of devastation.

"I hope some others managed to get away in time," I said staring at giant hole in the ground.

Within a second I noticed something was wrong. Inside the giant crater a shining white and blue gloss was spreading outwards across the land like a tidal wave.

The engine had stalled after the crash and Dalton was firing up the ignition trying to restart the vehicle.

"Yes, well, we have not quite evaded the situation ourselves just yet," Dalton explained as the engine burst into life with a weak roar.

While inspecting the destruction left behind by the explosion my heart sunk as I spotted something odd in the remaining forest. Where Malphas had been dragged back the trees were beginning to collapse in a straight line toward us ahead of the strange wave.

"He's coming back for us!" I shouted.

"What?" Jess questioned.

"Malphas! He mustn't have been caught in the explosion. He's comin back for us!" I pointed at the falling tree line.

Dalton instantly built up the pace following the road around the mountain. Remnant were once again on our tail not letting up for a single second now that they were clear of danger themselves.

As the ground began to rumble once more I heard helicopter blades whizzing through the air once more. Looking up to observe the location of the aircraft I noticed that it was not the illuminati's private copter but some other kind.

Driving around a long winding corner, more mechanical sounds began forming, closing in on our position. Remnant were right on us and before I could utter a word about the strange copter, Dalton decided to make a sharp turn off the road and into the steep decline through yet another forest.

Picking up a greater speed than before, the car rumbled across the uneven surface as Dalton tried his utmost to avoid the plant life. Shadows chased after us from the road above followed a minute later by the formidable Malphas. The chase seemed never ending, and the thought of an eventual capture was looming.

Suddenly bright lights cracked from behind the tree's ahead followed with the recognisable whistling of bullets flying in our direction.

"Jesus!" Dalton shouted above the increasing rate of gunfire. It took a second to realise that not a single shot had actually struck the vehicle but that the Remnant were slowly being picked off from all around us.

Outlines of men crouching by the trees were visible behind the flashes of gunfire.

"Who are they?" Jess asked the concentrating Dalton.

"I don't know, do I? Ask me again in a few minutes please!" he replied under stress.

"I don't think we should be worrying about them while this guy is still around!" I shouted forward indicating the fact that Malphas was once again right on top of us demolishing trees in his way. He seemed to have an extra livid expression on his face while the necklace of skulls floated around his chest.

Behind the enormous beast was a wave of blue frost covering the land The reversed fusion batteries explosion must be absorbing all the heat from the surrounding area – or something like that I'm no nuclear physicist – nevertheless it was catching up to fleeing Remnant, sticking them firmly to the ground as it passed.

Wheels and helicopter blades began exceeding the noise of the squealing engine occasionally disrupted by the hail of bullets.

"Oh my fucking god," I uttered as I continued to stare out the back window at Malphas who was almost within reach now.

"Woahhhh!" Came the unified yell of Jess and Dalton from the front followed by possibly the loudest bang I had ever heard from directly in front of us.

A large object was propelled at an extreme velocity directly into the shoulder of Malphas, completely tearing his arm off and ripping away a large section of his chest and sending him flying to one side whilst collapsing a tree in the process.

At the same time the car jerked quickly to the right. Stationary and just a few feet into the woods stood a large tank with a kind of squashed hexagonal turret aiming directly toward Malphas, its long barrel still smoking from the shot.

It almost seemed like the forest was coming alive around the tank until I received a clear view through the headlights that it was actually heavily camouflaged personnel closing in on the area. The relief which swept over me was immense, from doom and gloom to possible survival in a matter of minutes.

It was short-lived as the booming roar echoed through the dark forest from behind. Malphas rose up and charged down at the tank in a hail of gunfire whilst flashing in and out of existence. Standard weaponry seemed to do little to deter the beast from its path and it was only with the addition of extra gunfire coming from the skies which halted the monstrosity in its tracks.

Above us was the same helicopter I had seen before except now it was hovering above raining down a torrent of gunfire which sounded like an excessively angry swarm of bees. Malphas was being chewed to pieces by the flow of lead from all angles until once again with an ear shattering boom the tank tore a chunk straight from the centre of his chest. My eyes lit up with impressive display of military might against what was once a fearful foe.

He dropped to the floor reaching out with his remaining arm until finally giving in to the mortal wounds. The flood of frost had died down but still reached his body which chilled quickly before it phased over and over until disappearing out of existence. With that he was gone.

The leader of the Remnant was dead yet the danger was far from over as the remaining monsters swarmed at the tank which was doing a great job with the help of the camouflaged men in fending them off. Above the tree line the helicopter had focused its attention on the flying remnant gliding in circles around the vehicle.

Halting suddenly I lurched forward in the seat. In front of us four camouflaged men surrounded the car.

"AFARA!" one of the men shouted.

"Exit the vehicle everyone," Dalton instructed.

I pushed the door open and to my surprise it fell straight off the hinges and onto the dirt floor with a thud. Jess and Dalton also exited the vehicle as the disguised men cautiously approached. Everything was fine until Bill slowly showed himself. The men started shouting crazily and as I turned to look back the last thing I saw was the butt end of a rifle striking me directly between the eyes and falling onto a freezing cold floor.

Chapter 24

Revelations

In my mind I did not really dream. There were no imaginative nightmares or hopeful thoughts, more flashes of the past, memories of the events which had unfolded. There was no specific emotion involved in these thoughts as they skipped too quickly from one to the next, starting from the moment I spotted that flare emanating from that dreaded island, seeing the Remnant for the first time, meeting Jess, Bill and Zarathus, seeing a new world, being chased by the flying Remnant, Jaspers selfless death, waking up in hospital, meeting Dalton, trusting Ophanim, discovering a brotherhood of knights, watching the device implode and the death of a Remnant king of sorts. These things had all become a sort of normality in my life now.

Waking up I was still dazed and my eyes groggy. It took a few seconds to shake off the effects of being knocked out and focus on where I was. My first feeling was how cold it was, then scanning around I saw I was in a small square windowless room sitting on a basic steel seat with a steel table in front of me and another seat opposite. On the table were the pistol I had been using, the specialised torch given to me by Dalton and the small square radio device which had been stuck to my collar.

The floor was mirrored, perhaps so that the camera or an interrogator could see under the table and keep an eye on all angles. Staring down at myself I was covered in layers of blue and red blood mixed with mud, my hair was tattered and greasy and my face covered in a red graze from where I slid along the road. I smirked and looked back onto the table.

As well as my personal effects there was a laptop open and facing me. I moved my arm to inspect the laptop but was halted midway. Peering down to my sides I saw my wrists were chained down to the floor behind me, obviously someone was not very trusting of me. In the top left corner of the room a camera watched down at me with a little red light flashing underneath.

"Hello!" I shouted to the camera.

For some reason I wasn't worried. I felt like I probably should be worried or in the past I would have been but, right now, I felt OK. Even chained up I didn't feel like I was in danger, more like someone else thought that I was the danger.

No one came to greet me which I thought was a little rude. Perhaps I should do something to make them come to me. My device was still firmly attached to my arm which I pointed down to where the chain was clamped to the floor, the orange crosshairs lined up.

Fire.

Crack, Whistle.

With a sharp screeching noise the clamp crumpled in on itself as well as the metal floor leaving a hole digging deep into concrete underneath. My hands were now nice and free as the chain slid out of the cuffs. Moving my finger across the mouse pad the laptop came alive. The screen was black with a large play symbol placed in the centre. Obviously someone wanted me to see this anyway otherwise it would not have been put here in the first place. So I hit play.

A series of aerial photos and videos of the crater left behind in Bran played on the screen. Seeing the remains of the destruction from this angle was far more impressive than seeing it from the road as these images displayed the depth of the crater and compared it to the surroundings.

Following this were images of the Remnant, from the normal humanoid kind to the shadows of the flying kind. Videos of military personnel coming into close contact with the demonic monsters and even one clip of a man being violently possessed whilst surrounding men shouted wildly whilst shooting the creature.

After watching all the videos and images it became excessively clear that there was not going to be any way of covering this huge secret up much longer. It would be pretty difficult not to notice the giant perfectly formed hole in the ground where Bran once stood, showing no signs of nuclear fallout and a layer of frost. It was probably only a matter of time before the whole world would find out the truth. The consequences of this I could only begin to imagine.

While lost in my thoughts the door ahead of me clicked and slowly opened. In walked a tall man dressed in a full military uniform decorated with an array of medals. His hair was hidden under a military cap but his features were distinct – clean shaven, brown eyes, aged creases on his forehead and a strong jawline. Standing with a perfect posture with his hands behind his back he took a second to inspect me although I had no doubts he had probably been watching me through the camera and was only doing so to add an air of seriousness to his entrance.

Walking over to the seat he waited a second then pulled the seat out and slowly sat opposite me and shuffled in.

"Hello," I greeted casually, placing my hands on the table. I was a little surprised that he had not come in with any guards or any kind of weapon.

"Good evening, Griffin Holster," he replied in a clear and decisive English tone.

"Interesting video," I said pointing to the laptop quickly.

"It is certainly interesting to say the least," the man replied. "You could even go as far to say, life changing."

"You definitely could," I answered.

There was a second of silence and seriousness in the room as we sat watching one another.

"Who are you? Where are my friends and what do you want with me?" I asked while keeping firm eye contact.

"All your questions will be answered very shortly. As for now, I am General Thorburn and we have many things to discuss."

I would like to offer a special thank you to Rachel Victoria Gunby for producing yet again another outstanding piece of artwork for the front cover of the book!

Printed in the United States
By Bookmasters